WINTER'S KISS

STARLING BAY BOOK 1

SIENNA CARR

CONTENTS

Author's Note

Winter's Kiss is a STANDALONE romance in the *Starling Bay series*. This will be an on-going series of standalone romances based on different characters in this small coastal town.

While you do not need to read the books in order, it might enhance your reading experience if you do because each book is about a different couple, and a lot of the characters appear in different books. I also have a boxed set, **Escape to Starling Bay**, which features the first three books.

Starling Bay Series:

Whirlwind Kisses
Winter's Kiss
Maid for Him
Love Letters
Escape to Starling Bay (Books 1-3)
From Faking to Forever
Winter's Vow
Guarded Hearts
A Bouquet of Charm

Sign up for my newsletter and find out about new book releases:

http://www.siennacarr.com/newsletter/

CHAPTER 1

"*I* hate Christmas," cried Merry, "and Starling Bay—why would I want to go *there*?"

Her mother liked to interfere, but this was taking things too far. Merry felt better now. She *was* better. Of course, she worked a little too hard, but she had it all under control.

"To spend some quality time with your daughter, for one thing. And to get some rest. You've never stopped, Meredith," her mother pointed out. "Not even after Brian—"

"Don't, Mom." She didn't want the constant reminders.

"The doctor signed you off. There's no point in you moping around at home. You need to get away."

"But to Starling Bay? If I wanted a real vacation I'd go overseas."

"Would you?" Her mother gave her *that* look.

Okay. Maybe not. She hadn't gotten on a plane ever since Brian's accident. What should have been an exhilarating experience, a trip in a light Cessna aircraft, had turned into her worst nightmare when the engine caught fire. The plane burst into flames as it hit the ground ten minutes after take-off, killing both Brian and the pilot. She'd bought him the flying experience as a joint birthday and Christmas gift. Ever since then, she hadn't stepped foot inside a plane.

"You don't need to fly. You can drive."

"With Spartacus?" Their beloved Great Dane wasn't going to like the long road trip.

"You loved it when we used to go."

"That was years ago, Mom. I was a teenager then."

"And Chloe's a teenager now."

"The place is dead!"

Her mother returned a smug smile. "Apparently, no. It's booming. It was always a pretty little coastal town, but it's growing. I don't think I would like it so much now. Hyacinth tells me that it has undergone a lot of changes, but she still lives there, so it can't be all that bad."

Hyacinth Fitzsimmons was her mother's friend. Rather, her mother had made friends with the matronly woman the first time they had visited Starling Bay.

"Besides, they'll be getting ready for Christmas," her mother continued, "and I know how pretty it looks around this time of year."

"God, no," Merry groaned. *I hate Christmas.* She hadn't always hated it, only since Brian had passed away. He had loved it, and she had too, but spending it without him, especially that first time, just weeks after his passing, had been the hardest. From that moment on, she no longer looked forward to it. Christmas was about family, and being together, and being thankful, it was about feeling joyous and happy, and without her husband, she felt none of those things. The following year she couldn't bring herself to put up the tree, or buy gifts, or decorate the house. Luckily, for Chloe's sake, her parents had taken care of things.

"Meredith, it's about time you started to think more about Chloe." She lifted her face at her mother's stern tone.

2

"I *do* think about my daughter," she retorted. "It's not easy being a single parent."

"You want for nothing, I get that. You work hard, we see that. But your father and I also see that your daughter needs you. She doesn't need her grandparents as much as she needs you. Use this time wisely and spend it with her. Her school will be winding down in a few weeks' time. Why not take this opportunity and go away for a few months?"

"A few *months?*" She was thinking about the disruption to her daughter's schooling.

"Isn't that what your boss suggested? Thanksgiving's over and if you're that worried about school, you can always homeschool Chloe for a while. Spend quality time with your daughter for a change as well as taking a well-earned break for yourself."

Merry shook her head. Homeschooling sounded like hard work. She loved Chloe, but she had a feeling that her surly tween daughter would have to be dragged kicking and screaming all the way to a place where she knew no one. A place she had never been to. A place Merry herself hadn't been to for over a decade.

The idea was ludicrous.

Merry folded her arms. She had thrown herself into work after Brian's accident, and after the promotion, she continued to work crazy hours. Being the marketing manager for Boyd & Meyer, one of Boston's upscale department stores, came with a lot of pressure and responsibility. She had worked hard to get where she was, and the pressure was always on her to prove that she was worthy of that position, especially when resumes were always coming in from people who were so much better qualified than her on paper. She might not have had the degrees to prove it, but she could get the results that mattered.

The department store's sales had been increasing in recent years, and she liked to think that she had something to do with

3

this. Dan Shepworth, her boss and CEO, seemed to agree. He had been good to her.

The run-up to Christmas was one of the busiest times of the year, but something had happened to her in recent months. At first she'd thought it was nothing, her bouts of dizziness, and feelings of anxiety, but when these things became physical, when her hands became so clammy that she'd messed up her presentation to the management team, and when her blood pressure spiked, and she'd suffered a nosebleed, her parents had forced her to go to the doctor.

The doctor had prescribed rest and taking things easy. He advised her to take time off because she seemed to be on the brink of a breakdown if she continued her long hours.

It wasn't the work, or the pressure. She knew what it was. The five-year anniversary of Brian's death might have had something to do with it, and her cute, sweet daughter turning twelve might have pushed things over the edge for her.

"I can't afford to lose you, Meredith," Dan had told her a few weeks ago. "Take a couple of months off. You haven't had a good long break. Take time off, and come back when you're fit and ready."

He hadn't given her a choice. He had signed her off the week before Thanksgiving. But her first week at home hadn't been easy, either.

"Hyacinth could do with your expertise," her mother continued. "She's offered you one of the houses by the bay, you know, one of those pretty little places overlooking the oceanfront."

"She offered? When did she offer it?" Merry smelled interference.

"Oh, sometime last week."

She let out an irritated breath. She loved her parents, but her mother could be an interfering little soul. Merry knew her recent

4

health problems had scared her parents. It made them keep an even closer eye on her. They had moved all the way from California to Boston after Brian's death to be here for Merry and her daughter, and she was thankful for all they had done for her.

She also knew that her mother wasn't going to back down until she did what they suggested. "What am I going to do in one of those houses overlooking the ocean?" She would be bored out of her mind. Spartacus would be the only one who'd find any adventure in the move. She stared at the Great Dane who lay on his side, tongue lolling out, while she paced around the living room.

Her mother stepped in front of her, and gently took her by the shoulders. "This isn't just a difficult Christmas for you, it's hard on Chloe, too, seeing you looking down and not being well. She's so sensitive, given that she's on the brink of being a teenager."

"Don't I know it?" she muttered. Lately, her daughter had become more distant, preferring to stay in her room on her devices, or talking to friends on the phone. Merry knew it was her fault, that she had turned her back on her daughter in an attempt to come to terms with her grief. Brian's sudden passing had hit them like a train.

"I know it hasn't been easy for you, but don't think that it's been any easier for that girl. She was seven when Brian died."

"Don't, Mom." Merry looked away. Some Thanksgiving dinner this had turned out to be. Her father and Chloe were in the other room, her father asleep on the couch, and Chloe watching *Home Alone* for probably the tenth time.

It was time to take stock. Could she spend a few weeks, maybe even a month at Starling Bay? At least she'd get to spend Christmas away from Boston. That was an advantage worth considering. The malls and streets were already looking festive, and had been for the past month. She felt as if she'd stepped into Christmas the moment Halloween had ended.

5

"We want you back, Meredith," Dan Shepworth had told her. "I'm keeping this position open for you. Just get well, and come back." He reassured her that they would get by. She had a good team in place, and she would be in regular contact in case they needed her. Maybe a couple of months away would be good for her.

"Your boss might start thinking of replacing you, if you're not as sharp as you used to be." Her mother was oh-so-very clever. She had hit her right where it hurt.

Merry swallowed. Being considered not good enough by Mr. Shepworth, being replaced, would kill her.

"What do I have to do?" she asked, knowing full well that this casual conversation about Starling Bay was anything but casual. Her mother had a plan.

"Live in a beautiful home, enjoy Starling Bay, have quality time to yourself, get to know your daughter all over again. That's not too much to ask, is it?"

"What did you sign me up for, Mom? You said Hyacinth's letting me stay there for free. What's she expecting in return?"

"Nothing much."

"That doesn't sound like Hyacinth." She remembered her mother's friend as being a formidable woman who wore too much powder on her face.

"She could do with some of your marketing expertise, Meredith."

"*Marketing expertise*? I thought you wanted me to rest and take a break from the world of work."

"Oh, Meredith," her mother crooned. "Hyacinth is on the town committee, and she's leading the Christmas festivities. She only wants a few of your ideas and help."

"Ideas and help?" That job description was so vague as to be useless. But, compared to what her current workload would have been like at the department store, giving Hyacinth a few tips would be simple. She could do it with her eyes shut. "Okay. I'll go." At the very least it would get her mother off her back.

"Wonderful!" Her mother clapped her hands together and picked up the phone.

"What are you doing?"

"Calling Hyacinth to tell her that you're coming."

"When exactly does she expect me to come?" She hadn't thought about it, hadn't had time to get used to the idea.

"Next week, I expect. It's not long to go before Christmas."

Merry sucked in a breath, already regretting her hasty decision.

She hated Christmas.

CHAPTER 2

*D*ylan pulled the clay mugs out of the kiln and set them on a tray on the worktop.

Once they were glazed, he would paint them; wintery themes, Christmas trees, snowmen and snowflakes against the infamous backdrop of Starling Bay. He'd sell some here in his store and send the rest to The Gift Shop by The Bay, another gift shop in the center of town, which sold a good proportion of his handmade gifts.

He'd been hard at work all morning because he still needed to get on board with an order of vases which he was selling in a home furnishings store out of town. Slow and steady, that was his aim in increasing his sales.

Things could be better, but as long as income each year was steadily rising, he was doing well, at least, he thought he was.

His friends laughed and joked, asking him when he would start a 'real business', but he ignored them. Reed had inherited money, and Rourke was a savvy real estate broker. Dylan was an artist who was lucky enough to make a decent living from his art. It wasn't the kind of income that would attract gold diggers, and that, as far as he was concerned, was a blessing.

Not that he was looking to attract anyone these days. At thirty-five he considered himself too old to join the dating sites his friends pushed him to try. It was Rourke mostly, who pushed him, Reed, not so much

But he wasn't interested.

The sound of the bell tingling signaled the arrival of another visitor to his shop. He didn't rush to go out to the front knowing that Laura, his assistant, was already there.

"Where is that young man?"

His gut tightened. He was standing near the door of his workshop when Hyacinth's loud and distinctive voice carried over from the store. He was tempted to remain here, out of sight, and out of her way.

"He…he's busy…" He heard Laura say. His shop assistant was good, but she was no match for the formidable Hyacinth Fitzsimmons. Soon enough he knew she would be sniffing her way towards the back, and she would find him.

Muttering under his breath, he wiped his hands and decided to confront her. It was better to get this over and done with quickly.

"Hyacinth," he said, rubbing his hands together as he stepped into view. "You're on your yearly visit to see me."

"Nonsense," she threw back. "I come to your store when I have things to buy. I can see you've missed me." She wore a bright pink scarf and her face was already pink from a mixture of too much rouge and cold air. The coloring was way too bright for a woman of her years; she looked old enough to be his grandmother.

"*'Missed'* is probably the wrong word," he retorted.

"Then you must be *delighted* to see me." She gave him one of her annoying smiles.

"Wrong word again, what brings you here?" he asked, feigning ignorance. He knew perfectly why she had come.

"You know full well what brings me here, young man."

"I can't." He threw his hands up in front as if they were a protective shield.

"Can't? *Can't?* Don't be silly!" she cried. "There's no such word as 'can't' in my dictionary."

No. This wasn't happening. Not again. Not this year. "I can't do it," he replied, shaking his head.

"What do you mean you can't do it? Our one and only actor?"

"I'm not an actor," he said, growing increasingly exasperated. A failed actor, yes. If she wanted someone who could act, she should try asking Hailey Ross, Starling Bay's one and only claim to Hollywood fame.

"You're good enough."

He hung his head. *Good enough.* Turned out that good enough wasn't enough to pay the bills and rent. Luckily he'd been good with his hands, and had enough artistic talent to make a living doing *this*. The pageant had been fun the first couple of years, but he didn't want to be forever known as 'the guy who does the Christmas pageant.'

He had to get serious about his store, and his craft, and his pottery. He sold well enough, especially at Christmastime and the peak summer months, and combined with other places where he sold his products, meant that he did fine. But he could do better, and he needed to push himself to get his business to the next level. Also, the way things currently stood, he was slightly behind on his orders.

Directing Christmas pageants was not his life's ambition.

"We need you, Dylan. *Starling Bay* needs you. Don't let us down. If you can't do it, who will?"

"How about the priest? It's a *Christmas* pageant. Surely he should be your first port of call?"

"He's too busy, especially at this time of the year!"

"What about asking someone from his congregation?"

"Why ask them when we have a Hollywood star right here?"

That got his goat. He ground down on his molars. "I am *not* a Hollywood star, Hyacinth," he said, scratching the stubble across his chin. He needed to shave this thing off, but he'd been so busy in his workshop lately that he hadn't had the time.

The last thing he needed was to be accosted by Hyacinth. The woman was like a wart, hard, and unmoving.

"You're just being modest, Dylan," said Hyacinth.

"No," he insisted, pressing his thumb down on his temple. "I'm not."

"That isn't the answer I'm looking for."

His jaw turned to steel. He hadn't slept well lately, working late into the early hours trying to get caught up on his orders.

"I really don't need this, Hyacinth. I'm trying to expand my business and this…this… *pageant* isn't going to help me."

"Of course it will help you! How will it not? You'll get extra publicity for the event."

He wasn't buying it. Hyacinth was a master at putting her spin on things, and he wasn't going to be roped into it again.

Last year's pageant had been a nightmare. Joseph and Mary had had a spat on stage, and Baby Jesus hadn't stopped burping. Using a Baby Annabell Brother doll hadn't been a good idea; the cord had jammed and he hadn't been able to get up on the stage in time to fix it. The constant whining from the doll had thrown Mary and she had promptly forgotten all her lines. She'd stared at the audience blankly, until Joseph had taken the doll and smacked it face down on the floor. An eerie hush had then descended across the corner of the town square which was filled with proud parents and friends. A few seconds later, the crowd had burst out laughing.

No. He wasn't remotely interested in directing minors. He shook his head, refusing to be convinced otherwise. This year's Christmas pageant would have to take place without his input.

He. Was. Not. Doing. It. Again. He was determined to get through to her this time. "You're not listening, *Hyacinth*. I—"

"Oh," she said, taking out her bright pink woolen gloves. "Leah Shriver's offered to help out again."

And that was the best reason for not doing it. His heart plummeted at the mention of the name. Leah Shriver, a single mother, always offered to help out with the costumes and backstage stuff for the show. Because of this, she expected her son to always get one of the prime parts. Peter was now eleven years old, and was pleasant enough, so it hadn't been too difficult to give the boy a decent role. It was his mother who was the problem.

"She loves the Christmas pageant," Hyacinth gushed. "I wish you shared some of her enthusiasm."

"My enthusiasm is directed to my art, and my store."

Hyacinth exhaled loudly, then, "We have a corporate executive from one of the top department stores in Boston helping us out with the marketing this year. I'm sure I can ask her to help you out with this." She cast a slow glance around his store. He hadn't missed the slight upturn of her upper lip.

"It comes at a cost, however. If *you* direct the pageant, I'll make sure she puts you at the top of her list."

What was she talking about? "What list?" he asked, not understanding. "And who?"

"A friend's daughter. She's the marketing manager for a fancy-schmancy store in Boston and she's coming to Starling Bay to help us with marketing."

Why would someone from Boston want to come here and do *that?* He knew Hyacinth. Knew what a dragon she could be. She had probably coerced the poor woman into doing something she had no idea she had been volunteered for—just like he was about to be *'volunteered'* for directing this year's pageant.

Hyacinth lowered her head, and her voice. "She's coming to get away."

"From what?"

"It's this time of year, it brings back memories for her. She's a *widow.*" Hyacinth didn't say 'widow' but mouthed it, and for a moment Dylan almost thought she'd said 'window'.

"She lost her husband in a tragic accident a few weeks before Christmas, and this has always been a difficult time of year for her, apparently. Especially this year, it being the five-year anniversary. I'm doing her a favor."

He was too aghast for words. Trust Hyacinth to think she was doing that poor woman a favor.

"Besides," said Hyacinth, blinking rapidly. "Why would anyone *not* want to come here at this time of year? We attract a lot of tourists, you know. People go out of their way to visit our Christmas markets and to enjoy the glittering splendor of our town square. Starling Bay is fast becoming a go-to place for Christmas these days. So, be a good boy and direct the Christmas pageant, and I'll get her to help you out." Hyacinth winked at him, as if she had just procured a prestigious new contract for him.

It was true, he could do with some help. He didn't have time to put marketing things together. This could be worth a try. The pageant would take up a couple of hours a week, maybe a few weekends here and there, but if he got some expert marketing help, it would make it worth his while.

"Only this once, Hyacinth," he insisted. "This will be the last year I do this."

"Of course, young man," said Hyacinth, putting on her gloves and flexing her woolly pink fingers. "You said the same thing last year."

CHAPTER 3

"I hope you'll be happy here, Meredith," declared Hyacinth, as Merry climbed out of the car. "This is a beautiful home. I gave you one of the best. The elderly woman, whom Merry barely knew, beamed at her expectantly.

"Thank you for your kindness." Merry leaned in and gave her a stiff hug.

"Don't mention it, dear," Hyacinth continued. Merry stared at the woman's bright pink lipstick which was a tad too bright for a woman of her years.

Will I be happy here? Merry glanced up at the house with the door slightly ajar. The two-story home looked small, but cozy, with its pretty windows and brickwork.

"Thank you," Merry replied, though she would have been happy with anything. Money wasn't a problem. She had done well to support herself and Chloe.

"Goodness!" Hyacinth gasped, as Spartacus bounded out of the car. "What is that?"

"Spartacus," Chloe announced with glee. She stroked his face as the hound shook his head briskly. Merry could almost sense his relief to be outside again.

It had been a long journey and they'd had to stop every two hours to give the dog some fresh air. As a result, she was exhausted, because what should have been a five-hour trip had ended up taking almost seven hours.

"I didn't know you had a dog. Your mother never mentioned it." Hyacinth stared at Merry as if this was a huge problem. "Please make sure he doesn't break anything, or soil anything. I've given you one of my very best properties."

"So you keep saying," Merry muttered under her breath. But to the elderly lady she smiled sweetly and said, "I'll do that. Thank you very much, Mrs. Fitzsimmons." Chloe strode past with Spartacus. "Be careful with him, Chloe," Merry warned. Watching the Great Dane lolloping up the few steps to the house, he already seemed too big for it. She'd have to keep an eye on him and make sure he didn't break anything.

"I'm always careful," Chloe retorted, tightening her grip on his lead. "Easy boy. Is it okay for me to go in and look around?"

"I guess. Would it be okay, Mrs. Fitzsimmons?" Merry asked.

"It's *Miss,* and call me Hyacinth, dear, and yes. As long as your dog doesn't run around the house too much." Hyacinth's brow furrowed. "Maybe I should have given you one of my larger properties, further out? I have a barn which is shaping up nicely." She raised a hand to her chest and looked at them with trepidation.

"A barn?" Merry wrinkled up her nose. "He's a dog, Miss Fitz —Hyacinth. Not a farm animal."

"That's not what I meant, my dear. There's a new residential area that's just been developed, Forest Heights, not too far away. You'll need a car, mind you. A whole block of apartments has been built, and there are a handful of outhouses. They used to be barns and outbuildings before and they've turned them into these divine single one-story buildings. I've bought a couple of units for investment purposes, and I'm starting to think you might be better off there. It's surrounded by fields, and overlooks the forest, and there's even a lake."

Merry wasn't so sure. She liked the fact that this house was central to the town. "I'm sure this will be fine."

"It's not too late, if you'd like to move there," Hyacinth persisted. "Why don't you go and take a look tomorrow?" She rummaged through her handbag and pulled out a small brochure. "Forest Heights," she said, handing over the brochure. "Isn't it pretty? I could move you there next month if you prefer it."

Next month? "I'm not sure I'll be here that long," Merry replied quickly. She could live here for a few weeks, and had already made her mind up to return to Boston soon after Christmas. "But thank you for this." Merry glanced at the house. "It's very kind of you."

"It was the least I could do. Your mother said some time away would be good for you. How *are* you?" she whispered, her voice dropping to a somber, hushed tone.

"I'm fine, thank you."

Hyacinth peered at her closely, examining her face as if she was looking for something. Then she took her hand and patted it. "It must have been awful, you being widowed so young, and your poor daughter." She shook her head. "Starling Bay will give you all the rest and recovery you need. A nervous breakdown is a terrible thing."

"I didn't have a nervous breakdown," Merry shot back. She withdrew her hand from Hyacinth's. Her mother should have known better than to broadcast everything to this woman. "It was a bout of anxiety and working too hard. I'm not ill, Miss Fitzsimmons. I'm really not."

"Of course not, dear," said Hyacinth, but everything about her expression and her voice indicated otherwise.

"We're going to take a look upstairs," Chloe shouted from the

16

door. Merry nodded, her stomach tight with anxiety. "I'd better start unpacking," Merry said, hoping that Hyacinth would leave.

"I hope you will be happy here, dear."

"I'm sure we will."

Merry hoped for her sake and Chloe's that she would, too. It was nothing like the home she lived in; the home she had once shared with Brian. Memories were everywhere, and lately she had been prone to getting down about it all. Five years down the line, she had accepted his passing but being a single parent was so hard, and juggling her hectic work life with a surly daughter was becoming harder.

"Would you like me to show you around?"

"Uh…" Spartacus was usually excited when he was in a new place. It was probably better not to. "No, I think we'll be fine, thank you."

"Very well. Spend the next few days exploring the town. You still remember it, I suppose?"

Merry nodded. "But I haven't been back for years. Not since I was at school."

"There are still some places that have been here for decades. You might remember them, but a lot of it has changed. Unfortunately, a lot of new places have sprung up." Hyacinth shook her head, looking pained. "Why do things have to change?" she mumbled to herself. "I'll leave you to it, dear." She turned to walk away.

"When do I …start?" asked Merry, hesitating. She wasn't sure how to phrase it. Hyacinth had allowed her to stay here rent-free for a few months, not that money was an issue, but she sensed her mother had had something to do with getting her carted off to Starling Bay.

"We have a meeting in the town hall next week, on Wednesday at 7:00 p.m. You should come to that."

"I should?" What had happened to her rest and recovery?

17

"I'll call to remind you. We have regular meetings, but this one is with most of the shop owners and business people. They will be most interested to meet you."

"They will?"

"They can't wait. I will introduce you to everybody then."

A knot twisted in Merry's gut. A formal meeting, in the town hall, with business people? It didn't sound at all like how she had imagined spending her rest and recovery time.

"How…how many people?"

And what exactly do I need to do?

She'd been thinking that it would be informal; that Hyacinth would introduce to her a couple of people. Never in her wildest dreams had she envisaged a meeting of this scope, and at the town hall of all places.

"Oh, all the business owners, dear. Everyone in Starling Bay knows me."

"But is it necessary for me to meet *everyone?*"

"Of course! They will want to meet *you.* And why wouldn't they when we have the services of a marketing expert from Boston at our disposal."

"I'm not sure…this isn't…I was supposed to be taking a break." A feeling of helplessness washed over her, and she sensed that she was getting pulled in deeper and deeper into something she hadn't signed up for.

"This is Starling Bay, Meredith. Not Boston. Life is lived at a slower pace here, you'll see. You'll only have to do a few consultations here and there. It's not a bad deal, is it? Look at the beautiful home you're getting in return. You help me and I help you. It's business and friendship, an irresistible combination."

It wasn't quite what she'd had in mind when she'd set off for Starling Bay, and now it was too late to turn around and head back. Driving away from Boston had been freeing. Something about that city, and Christmas, did something to her. Images about Brian and that horrific accident swirled in her head.

She was here now, and she would do her best.

But what was she supposed to do about Chloe? Back in Boston she could leave Chloe and go off. Go shopping or work late, and not worry about her daughter because her parents would be on hand to take care of her.

Here in Starling Bay she had no one.

"Where and with whom am I supposed to leave my daughter for these 'little' marketing consultations?"

"I'll get my housekeeper to come over and keep an eye on her."

"But what if—" My daughter doesn't like your housekeeper? She refrained from saying her thoughts out aloud because it didn't show Chloe in a good light. Instead, she asked, "But I don't know your housekeeper. She could be anyone."

"Your mother knows her."

"My mother?"

"Call her and ask her about Joan."

Merry stared back at the older woman and felt as if she'd been steamrolled into leaving Chloe with a stranger. "I'll do that."

"Don't worry, Meredith. You're going to get the break you need. You'll only have to have the odd meeting here and there."

Merry closed the door and wondered how worried she should be.

CHAPTER 4

"I'm bored. There's nothing to do here."

Merry inhaled deeply, letting her daughter's words hang in the air. "That's the whole point, Chloe. We're supposed to do nothing. No school for you, no work for me."

"But it's boring. Can I have my iPad back?"

"*Please,*" Merry said. "The magic word is please."

"Please," her daughter parroted.

"You can, but not yet."

Chloe stomped her foot on the ground. Merry stared at her in disgust. "You really did that?" she asked. "You're really having a tantrum here on the street?"

Chloe folded her arms and stared back defiantly. "A boring cup of hot chocolate in a boring old town isn't fun. I wanna go home to my friends."

Merry blew out a breath. She wasn't going to give in. She gripped Spartacus's lead tighter in her hand. The dog stood by obediently, caught in the middle of their standoff.

Where had she gone wrong?

She already knew the answer, even as she dwelled on it. She worked so hard to make sure her daughter had everything she ever wanted; the latest device, the newest clothes. It dawned on her that she had been so focused on buying Chloe anything she wanted, and even then her daughter was so moody and ungrateful.

Today had been new for them. A new routine, a new home, a new place. A new dynamic between them. Today she didn't have to go to work and leave Chloe at Breakfast Club at school, and this evening she wouldn't be coming home late just in time for dinner. Though there were many days she didn't get back until after dinner, days when her parents stepped in to help her out.

Today had been different because she and Chloe had had the entire day to themselves. Boy, had it been difficult. They had wandered around the town with Spartacus, taking a look at the shops and restaurants along the bay and the surrounding areas. Later, after visiting the town square they'd even had a hot chocolate in one of the small dining places.

"Look at that Christmas tree," she said, trying to get Chloe interested in something. A tall pine tree stood smack bang in the middle of the town square.

"This is boring." Chloe's mouth twisted, then clamped shut.

"If you're that bored, I can give you some math to do, and after that you can do some English comprehension," Merry snapped.

Chloe made that noise again—a sound that Merry had become accustomed to. A loud exasperated sound as if doing anything was too much trouble. "Do that again, and I will double your workload."

"That's not fair!"

Why did her daughter do nothing but complain all day long? Merry tried hard to keep her anger in check, but this was new to her as well. Usually she would have left the house and after dropping her daughter off at school, she'd go to work, doing long hours which took up most of the day and ate into the evening.

"What's not fair?" she asked. "We're on an adventure." She'd told herself that this was what it was, and that Brian would have been proud of her.

"I don't want an adventure. I want my friends, and my bedroom, and my life back," Chloe whined.

Merry didn't want to address this. Didn't want to deal with it right now. Something deep in her core reminded her that things hadn't been like this always. They'd been happy once, and Chloe had been an adorable child back then, when Brian was still around. When there had been someone else to share the load, back when they had been a family.

"I want to go back home."

"We're here now, and we're going to make the most of it."

"Then I want to go back to the house," said Chloe.

But Merry didn't relish the idea of going back home and sitting indoors for the rest of the day, either.

"We're not going back, we're staying out," she announced suddenly. "Do you want to go for a run, Spart?" Spartacus's eyes lit up, and his tongue lolled out, and his panting grew faster. Her daughter could stay bored, but Spartacus was excited.

"Go for walkie?" Merry asked him again, watching his tail waggle.

They would go and take a look at the new housing development, and the fields where Spartacus could go for a run. The poor dog had been cooped up in the Jeep on the journey yesterday, and Merry could tell he was itching to run wild.

"You choose, Chloe," she said, folding her arms and not backing down. "Either you come with me and Spartacus, or you can go home and do some work. What will it be?" She examined her daughter's face and waited for that same sigh of exasperation. When none was forthcoming, she felt as if she'd won a tiny battle. "Let's go."

They returned home, then got into the car. Starling Bay was

small enough to walk around in, but this housing development that Hyacinth had mentioned was a short car ride away.

Driving past fields and greenery, they left the town behind them, and she saw in the distance what looked like a row of wooden cabins. On driving closer, she saw the signpost. It was for Clearwater Village, and then beyond that, the place Hyacinth had mentioned, Forest Heights.

Merry decided to park and take a look around here first. The housing area wasn't something she was particularly keen to visit, because she had already decided to stay in Starling Bay. She just had to make sure that Spartacus didn't break anything.

Chloe got out of the Jeep first, and let Spartacus out, while Merry looked over Hyacinth's brochure. She was trying to get her bearings for the forest, and saw that there was also a lake nearby when she heard the commotion. And then she heard Chloe's loud rebuke.

"No, Spartacus, nooooooooooooo….."

Merry turned to see Chloe being dragged along by an unrestrained Spartacus. The dog surged ahead, yanking her daughter along with him. He was too big, but he was well trained, so something must have caught his attention.

Merry ran towards them, wishing she had grabbed his lead from Chloe right from the start.

She saw the door open, and a woman walked out with two bags in her hands. She seemed startled at the sight of Spartacus but quickly moved past him.

Merry breathed a sigh of relief.

Until she saw Spartacus charge into the shop like a demon on legs., and then her heart plummeted.

CHAPTER 5

*H*e was annoyed. He was so annoyed that he didn't feel like working today, but he knew he had to. And he always loved locking himself away in his workshop and being left alone.

But Hyacinth Fitzsimmons had steamrolled over his objections yesterday, and he hadn't slept a wink last night. He should have been stronger. He should have pushed back. Neither Reed nor Rourke would have put up with this.

Hyacinth was a big, bold and brash woman, and she simply did not understand the meaning of the word 'no.'

"I'll be in the back," he told Laura, then flashed a smile at the smartly dressed couple who were looking around the store. He decided to stay a while and see if they needed assistance. A couple dressed like that wasn't from around here. He knew, not only because of the way they dressed, but also because his customers were mostly made up of tourists to Starling Bay, and not the locals so much.

Besides, more and more people were venturing out to Clearwater Village, a small community of artists and shops that weren't commercial enough, or stupid enough, to pay the high

24

rents that the areas around the bay commanded. It was on the way to Forest Heights—a new development of luxury apartments and single one-story homes which overlooked one end of the lake.

His friend Reed had invested heavily in the project and was no doubt getting a serious return on it, while his other friend, Rourke, was making good commission out of showing people properties and convincing them to buy. The apartments were luxurious and expensive. And completely out of his budget.

Starling Bay attracted many tourists, and this new development, Dylan hoped, would ensure that this enclave of shops would get a boost in visitor numbers.

"Hi there," he said, nodding his head and smiling at the couple. The man's Rolex watch was hard to miss. He flashed another smile, and couldn't help but stare at the woman's bag. Peeking out from the top of it was what looked like a toy dog. But then its head moved, and Dylan realized that it was a dog. No bigger than his hand. Not a guard dog, but a dog that was more of an accessory, as far as he was concerned.

This was the type of couple who usually left with bags of gifts. "Is there anything I can help you—" But before he could finish his sentence, the shop door slammed wide open and something resembling a horse charged towards him.

He heard the crash, saw his new Christmas coffee cup collection in pieces on the floor, and his heart choked up in his throat.

What in the world was this?

He heard the tiny dog-in-the-bag whimper, and he rushed towards the entrance, seeing his beautiful mugs lying in pieces on the floor. Anger knotted up his airways and he almost forgot to breathe.

"They're broken," whined Laura as she crouched down to inspect the damage. Dylan turned his attention to the beast.

"*Nooooo*! Spartacus. NOOOOOOO!" A child raced in.

Surprisingly the creature was on a leash but the girl holding the leash looked not much bigger than the beast itself.

His eyes narrowed. Where was the owner?

Laura gasped loudly. "Goodness, no!" She crouched on the floor to pick up the pieces.

Anger roiled in Dylan's gut.

This was a first.

Nothing like this had happened here before.

Ever.

He stomped towards the door, looking for a responsible adult, until WHAM! Something collided into his chest. Something soft, leaving a scent of roses. It was a woman. She sprang back in shock, her eyes wide, her lips parted. For a moment she reminded him of a bird. She stumbled back, a shocked moan escaping her lips. His mouth fell open and he didn't know whether to be angry or to ask her how she was.

"Chloe!" the woman cried, suddenly turning her gaze to the child.

"What happened?" She looked around, the color draining from her face, as shock spread across it. "Chloe!" He heard the desperation in her voice as she took the beast's lead from the girl

"I didn't know he was going to do—"

The woman looked around, her gaze running over the table knocked onto its side and the broken pieces of pottery on the floor. "Oh my goodness, he's broken everything."

Woof, woof!

The hound growled, and the woman grabbed the lead with both hands. "Spartacus, NO!" she yelled. "NO." The dog didn't move.

The well-dressed couple walked around the other side, deftly avoiding the mess which was right in the middle of the shop.

"We have other things you might like to look at," Dylan offered, hoping to entice them to stay.

26

"We'll come back another time," the woman replied, but Dylan knew the chances of that were slim.

The tiny little dog in the bag yelped. So that was what had set the beast off. Behind him, Dylan heard it growl again. His nostrils flared. Not only had that thing damaged his display, but he'd also scared off what might have been good customers.

"Please keep a tight rein on your leash," he said to the woman he presumed was the dog's owner, and the girl's mother.

"I am so, so sorry." She stared at the floor in dismay.

"They were new mugs." Dylan eyed the dog—if it could be called a dog—with trepidation, before lifting his gaze to his broken wares, and the mess. He saw the worried look on the young girl's face. She was pale.

"I'm really sorry." Her voice was low, and full of remorse. "He yanked the lead and I couldn't …"

Dylan's anger subsided a little. "Your mom should have taken control of the lead." It was hardly the girl's fault. He glanced over his shoulder to see that the girl's mother had crouched down and was picking up the broken pieces with Laura.

She stood up with fragments of broken mugs in her hand. "I'm so sorry. Where do you want me to put these?"

"The bin is over here," he said walking towards the main desk with the point-of-sale counter. He opened the trash bin and threw them in. "I'd only made them a few days ago."

"*You* made them?" the young girl asked.

"Yes."

"I'm really sorry," her mother repeated.

"A dog like that needs to be kept on a tight rein, especially in a gift shop like this. He shouldn't have been in here in the first place."

"You don't have a sign up saying dogs aren't allowed," the woman retorted. There was a sharp edge to her voice. "That other couple brought their dog in."

"Their dog wasn't the size of an elephant."

"He's hardly the size of an elephant." She looked visibly upset, but he didn't care, and he wondered how she would react if he'd done something like that to her home. It was going to take the better part of tomorrow to make new mugs, and with the pageant taking up a large chunk of his time over the busy Christmas period, he wasn't happy at all.

"I'll pay for it," she said, pulling out her purse.

Yes, you will, he thought, somewhat relieved. "That will be $110, please." He'd already done a quick estimate of the damage.

The woman's eyes widened in disbelief. "$110 for a handful of cups?"

"They're handmade."

She handed over the bills.

"There's a sign as soon as you step inside saying that you have to pay for anything that you break—"

"I'm not complaining about having to pay."

"It sounded like a complaint to me." He handed her the receipt.

"I don't need this," she said, scrunching up the flimsy paper in her hand.

"Feel free to look around. We've got many other things in the store if you—"

"No, thank you." She didn't look too happy.

"Hopefully we'll see you next time when you'll have him on a —"

"I heard you the first time," she said, "and the second and third time. He'll be on a leash. He *was* on a leash."

Dylan forced himself to smile. He wasn't sure why he felt tight, on guard, defensive. The beast's owner hadn't shirked from paying for the damage, and she'd apologized many times, but something about her had rubbed him the wrong way, and clearly, something about him was doing the same to her.

Maybe he'd just lost his touch with women. Not that he was trying to hit on this one. She was pretty, he thought. All eyes, and lips. Married too, and therefore clearly off the menu. "Then you'll have to be the responsible adult and make sure he doesn't run wild in another store next time."

Her lips twisted, and it seemed as if she was trying hard to hold back from saying something. "Come on, Chloe." She turned her back to him.

"Aww, mom, can I have a look around?"

"Here? Are you sure?"

His eyes narrowed. What was wrong with *here?*

"I just want to look around. They've got food bowls for Spartacus."

"We can get those made with his name on it, too, if you want," said Dylan, stepping away from the till. He was surprised at his own offer, but he felt sorry for the child.

"You can?" The girl's face brightened. Her mother folded her arms.

"Please, Mom. *Please. For Christmas.* I'll get Spart one for Christmas."

"You can place an order, and I'll have it ready by next week," he said, hoping to appeal to her mother.

"Okay." But she seemed not-too-happy about that.

Dylan wondered why he was offering this. He didn't usually offer to make custom-made dog bowls, but since he was going to have to make a new batch of mugs, he could just as easily make a whale-sized one for the beast with the whale-sized name.

"Could I have one like this, in red, with his name across the front?"

"Sure." He pulled out a notebook and wrote it down. "If you come by in a week's time, it will be ready."

"Do you want me to pay you now?"

He shook his head. "You can pay when you pick it up."

"I'm going to look at some other things, Mom."

"Don't take too long, Chloe. I'll be outside with Spart."

"We have some cool Christmas gifts," he said, making an effort to be nice. She was a customer, after all, and she had paid for the damaged goods, and her daughter was placing an order for a dog bowl.

"I'd rather not risk my dog trashing your store again."

"He's a big dog," he remarked, attempting to make conversation.

"My husband picked him. He wanted a big guard dog for the family."

"Can't fault his way of thinking." He took a step backwards, eager to return to his workshop at the back. "I'll have that bowl ready by next week."

"I heard you."

CHAPTER 6

*M*erry clamped her lips together, determined not to have an outburst and say something she might regret. Anger simmered slowly inside her. How was it that her twelve-year-old could wind her up so much? When had this happened?

"Can you please just sit here through this meeting?" Merry hissed. What was she doing here, on a Wednesday evening, at the town hall? She looked around the room which was full of people. There were rows of seats at the front and a small stage, she prayed she wouldn't have to get up there and be introduced to everyone. She took a deep breath, then another one.

This wasn't Chloe's fault. It was her mother's fault and Hyacinth's.

"I'm sorry, Chloe. I have to do this, please can you try and get through it for my sake?"

"Why did you have to drag me here?" Chloe whined.

"Because I didn't want to leave you home alone."

"You used to leave me home alone before."

Merry turned to her daughter sharply. "You were never alone. Grandma and Grandpa were always there."

"*You* weren't."

Defiance flashed in her daughter's eyes. Merry understood the resentment. It dripped out of Chloe in fits and starts, but now was not the time to have *that* discussion. "Miss Fitzsimmons wanted to—"

"She said to call her Hyacinth."

"Could you please just sit here quietly? Can you do that for me, just this once?"

"You don't always make it to my meetings when I ask you to come."

So this was about *that?* "I missed your last parents' evening because I was away at a workshop, Chloe. I couldn't help it," she said through gritted teeth.

She didn't want to be here herself. The entire week so far had been trying on her nerves. Chloe hated it with a vengeance, and after that nightmare episode at the pottery store, things had never gotten any better.

Merry longed to be back at work, slaving over her desk and working long hours in her office again. And having her parents look after Chloe. They seemed to handle her better.

Why, oh why, oh why had she allowed herself to get roped into coming to Starling Bay?

Why had she listened to her mother?

"There you are!" Hyacinth's loud voice cut across the chattering in the room. "Come along, Meredith. There are several people interested in meeting you."

"Now?" Wasn't the meeting about to start? Sweat formed along Merry's hairline at the back, and she blinked. Her heart began to race. This was just like before, when she'd felt dizzy, when her hands had turned sweaty and she couldn't focus on the task at hand. She was supposed to be over that.

"Come along," quipped Hyacinth. "Hurry."

Merry stood up slowly.

"What am I supposed to do?" Chloe asked.

"Wait here."

"I could have waited at home."

Merry looked around the large room full of people. At the front half, before the stage, were rows of chairs. "Go and sit at the front, where I can keep an eye on you. Please, Chloe," she begged. "I'll come back as soon as I can."

Her daughter huffed out a breath loud enough for the people nearby to hear, then walked away.

Tonight was going to be a stressful evening. She could already feel the tension in her neck. Smoothing down her hair, she followed Hyacinth who cut through the crowd of people with ease.

"This is the marketing expert we have on loan to us," Hyacinth announced, as she came to a stop near a group of people. "This is Meredith Nicholls." They all turned to her with smiles, and it wasn't long after that the questions came. They needed help with marketing, and wanted to know how to use social media, how to find their audience.

With a subtle nod, Hyacinth left her and Merry answered questions as best as she could, while making sure that she didn't get too involved and made no promises. After half an hour of talking, she was completely worn out. She hadn't meant to talk so much, but these people seemed to hang onto her every word.

"Starling Bay needs someone like you," one of them said.

"Thank goodness Hyacinth managed to get you over here," someone else said.

"If anyone can, Hyacinth can," someone to her left said.

"I'm only here for a month, if that," Merry replied, wanting to set their expectations right.

"Hyacinth said you were going to help us with our Christmas push."

"It's a bit late for that—" Merry replied.

33

"It's never too late."

The room started to hush as Hyacinth got on the stage and tapped the microphone.

"Please take your seats," she boomed. "We are ready to start." And just like that people flocked towards the empty chairs. Meredith excused herself and walked to the front row where Chloe was sitting, engrossed on her cell phone.

"Please put that on silent."

"Why? I'm bored."

"Because I'm asking you to."

Chloe ground out an exaggerated moan and begrudgingly put the cell phone away. Merry barely had time to sit back when Hyacinth's words made her pay sharp attention. "I have managed to woo over a marketing expert. She is the Marketing Manager of Boyd & Meyer in Boston. Some of you will have been lucky enough to have met her by now. I have mentioned to some of you that she will be helping us with our Christmas drive this year, so without further ado, please welcome to the stage, Meredith Nicholls."

Merry's heart almost shocked right out of her chest. She hadn't expected this, and she hadn't prepared a speech.

"She never said I'd have to go up there," she muttered under her breath. For a few moments, she sat there in shock, her body locking up.

"Mom!" Chloe whispered loudly. "Go up. They're waiting."

"Come along now, Meredith," Hyacinth commanded.

Merry stood up. She heard the rush of blood pounding through her ears as she forced herself to walk up the four steps to the stage. She gave Hyacinth a what-am-I-supposed-to-say death stare because while she was used to speaking in front of crowds, she was so ill-prepared for this.

And then she heard a cell phone start to ring from somewhere in front. It sounded familiar, but she could taste the bile in her throat, and the ringing became background noise.

What on earth was she supposed to say?

For a moment, she felt like crying. Or shouting, or telling the audience there had been a terrible mistake.

She didn't want this. She didn't want to be up here, in front of a crowd of people she didn't know, giving them a speech that she was ill-prepared for.

Hyacinth crossly took the mic again. "Whose phone is that?" she thundered.

Oh my goodness.

Merry's stomach heaved. It was her phone.

She tried to catch Chloe's attention but her daughter was happily texting away on her own cell phone, and seemed unfazed, or was too distracted to notice the ringtone. All eyes were on Merry, and her gaze flickered quickly across the crowd, and then stopped.

On *him.*

The guy from the store was there, and he was sitting with a couple of other guys, grinning.

He was laughing at her.

She felt all eyes on her and thought she heard whispers dart around the room like spear-headed missiles.

In that moment, their gazes locked, and the smile slipped from the gift-shop owner's face.

It was proof enough that she'd caught him red-handed.

She took the mic. "Chloe," she said, trying to soften her voice, and smiling, "Please would you turn my cell phone off." Chloe looked up at the mention of her name, and did as she was told.

Merry stared at the crowd, and forced herself to avoid looking at that obnoxious store owner who was obviously having a laugh at her expense.

Butterflies skittered around in her belly, but she was

determined to put things right. She'd done this before. She could do this now, even being as unprepared as she was. She was a professional and she was over that illness.

She was.

"I'm sorry, I didn't know I was supposed to make a speech. Miss Fitzsimmons didn't tell me, so I'm going to have to wing it."

The audience laughed, and Merry's shoulders relaxed a little.

CHAPTER 7

"It was the size of an elephant," said Dylan when he'd finished recounting the tale of the beast that had burst into his store last week.

"It can't have been," Reed replied, calmly.

"It was."

"Get real," Rourke exclaimed. "You exaggerate too much."

"You'd agree with me if you saw the damn thing." He told them how the hound had all but demolished his new collection of coffee mugs. Come to think of it, the owner hadn't come back to pick up the custom-made dog bowl.

"Your entire collection of cups gone?"

"Not all of them, but enough to annoy me."

"But she paid?"

"She did." She'd been good about it. He hadn't even had to ask her.

"Drinks later?" asked Rourke, dropping his voice. Dylan nodded. He was up for it.

"I can't," Reed replied, looking glum.

"You never can, ever since you got engaged," Dylan complained. "We hardly see you."

Reed made a face. "I see you guys every week. I'm seeing you right now, aren't I?"

"Then what are we doing here? We should be sitting in a bar." Rourke looked to him for backup. "Let's go. It's not too late."

"We can't leave now," Dylan growled. It would be impossible to tiptoe out of the hall especially with Hyacinth on the stage. Her beady eyes never missed a thing. Hyacinth Fitzsimmons had practically bullied him into attending tonight's meeting. She seemed to go into monster mode as soon as December started. "She's supposed to introduce me to some marketing expert," he told them.

"Lucky you," Rourke remarked. "You should pass her over to me. I'm sure I'll make better use of her *advice*, since you'll be busy with the pageant."

His friends roared with laughter.

"Don't," said Dylan. He watched Hyacinth get up on the stage and tell everyone to take their seats.

"Too late to leave now," complained Rourke as a hush fell over the entire room.

"I can't leave anyway," Dylan groaned.

"And I can't go out," Reed stated.

"Olivia has you on a leash, lover boy," crooned Rourke. "Say, when are you going to get her to invite me to one of her parties?"

"How desperate are you?" Dylan asked, incredulous.

"What?" Rourke shot back. "If I'm lucky enough to have a friend who's engaged to a beauty queen, I should make the most of it."

"*Ex*-beauty queen," Reed clarified.

Shush. Someone behind them made a loud disapproving noise and the three of them hushed up quickly.

Dylan twiddled his thumbs, and looked around. The room was packed. Hyacinth had managed to get everyone to attend so that she could preside over them like a queen bee. Wouldn't it have been better to have had this meeting a couple of months ago? Starting the Christmas marketing push for Starling Bay now, in the first week of December, was pretty lame, in his opinion.

He had only come tonight because of Hyacinth's promise to him, and he hoped that the marketing expert from Boston was here. He was all for free marketing advice.

"I have managed to acquire the services of a marketing expert," he heard Hyacinth say, and he looked up then almost choked. "It can't be."

"What?" Rourke asked.

Shush! The same person behind them made a disapproving noise.

Reed nudged him in the ribs. "What's the matter?"

Hyacinth's voice boomed from the stage. "Without further ado, please welcome to the stage, Meredith Nicholls." He watched the owner of the hound who had crashed into his shop walk up the stairs.

"No way." He gasped. *She* was *her?* The cold-as-ice owner of the beast? And then it hit him. She was a widow. That's what Hyacinth had said. And she had come here to get away.

"Hey," said Rourke, elbowing him again. "What's wrong with you? You look like you've just seen your ex."

He would recount this comment later, and note that seeing his ex no longer impacted him as much. But *this*. This was a surprise. "It's her," he said, his voice flat as he watched Meredith take the microphone.

"She's the expert from Boston?" Reed asked. Dylan nodded, and Rourke made an approving noise which Dylan didn't like.

"She's pretty," his friend said. "Put in a word for me, would you? Better still, introduce her to me."

"Get lost," Dylan replied, his throat drying up. He couldn't help but stare at her, especially since she hadn't seen him yet. His mind recalled that moment when she'd bumped into him, she'd

39

come rushing through the door and slammed straight into him. Something had flashed behind those amber-colored eyes when she'd stepped back, startled. She *was* pretty, there was no disputing the fact.

"Her dog broke my Christmas mugs," he said. "And all because he was chasing a rat-sized dog in a bag."

"A rat-sized dog? You sure it wasn't a gerbil?" Rourke laughed.

"It was a dog."

Reed chortled, and just at that moment, the marketing expert from Boston stared directly at him. Her hard stare stopped his smile and he turned somber.

Somewhere, a cell phone was going off, and the woman, this Meredith Nicholls, grew flustered. It looked as if she'd lost her train of thought. It looked as if she was genuinely stuck, and suddenly he felt sorry for her.

CHAPTER 8

This was hell on earth. Her short speech on the stage had gone smoothly, especially when she had managed to successfully block that odious man out of her mind. That smirking store owner and his friends had been laughing at her. She was sure of that. After a brief introduction of what she did, and her honesty in saying she wasn't sure what Hyacinth had in mind for her, Meredith left the stage with relief, glad to be back in the comfort of her seat.

She listened as Hyacinth addressed the audience and told them about upcoming events. There was a Christmas pageant taking place, and all sorts of activities going on in the town in the run up to Christmas. She clocked off halfway, and felt sorry that she had dragged her daughter along to this.

Later, when Hyacinth sat down, there was a general question and answer session with the committee members and the rest of the audience.

Merry looked around, trying to assess her chances of making a discreet exit, but sitting at the front of the hall made it impossible. She was forced to sit and listen to events which meant nothing to her.

When the meeting was finally over, she grabbed Chloe's hand. "Let's go," she said, standing up to rush off, but she was accosted by people along the way. They were interested in seeking her services, and many wanted to know if they could have a consultation with her at some point.

She shouldn't have trusted her mother. When something sounded too good to be true, it usually was. Why had she ever accepted this deal? She didn't need a rent-free apartment, and would have happily paid. Money had never been an issue, even after Brian's death.

"I can't believe I let that woman bully me into doing something I didn't want to do," she groaned. "Springing that speech on me when I had nothing prepared."

"You weren't so bad, Mom."

She looked at her daughter in surprise. "No?"

Chloe shook her head. "Nobody freaked out about it as much as you did."

Merry let out a laugh. "I did not freak out."

"You looked like you wanted to die."

They fell silent.

"Sorry, Mom." Chloe looked down at her feet. Merry put her arm around Chloe's shoulder. "Sorry for what? You don't need to apologize." Certain words still felt as uncomfortable as barbed wire. "Let's get out of here."

The meeting was officially over, but everyone stood around in groups talking. She was eager to make a quick exit before more people came up to her to ask her how she could help their businesses.

"Did you want to sign up for the Christmas pageant?" she asked Chloe. It suddenly occurred to her that it might be a way of getting her daughter involved in something while she was here, especially since she was missing out on school for a while. It would keep her busy.

"Ewww, no way."

"It might be fun."

"Nothing here is fun."

"Is it really that bad?" Merry asked, listening to Chloe properly for the first time. They walked past a row of tables set up with refreshments. "Grandma thought it might be good for us to get away, you know, for Christmas and all that."

And all that.

Merry stopped and faced Chloe, then placed her hands on her daughter's shoulders. "If you want to go back home, we can go home."

Chloe stared up at her with big brown eyes. Brian's eyes. Each time she looked at her daughter, she was reminded of him. It was bittersweet.

Chloe shrugged.

"If you really hate it here, we can go home."

"You like it here," Chloe retorted.

Merry blinked, puzzled as to what might have given Chloe that impression. In a way, it had helped her to be away, to not be in the house filled with happier memories of life before. But Christmas would suck wherever she was, because each year it was a reminder of Brian's passing, and therefore no longer something she looked forward to. Her parents and friends continually told her that Chloe was young and that she had to make it fun again for her daughter, but each year she found that she couldn't do it.

"I don't *not* like it here."

"You seem more calm," said Chloe.

"Calm?"

"You're not rushing around, and you're not at work. You didn't even get really, really mad when Spart broke into that shop."

She nodded, agreeing. Uptight Merry would have exploded.

"Spart broke into that shop," she repeated, the memory of that time making her smile.

Chloe started to laugh.

"He sounds like a bandit, doesn't he?" Merry remarked, grinning.

"Excuse me," someone tapped her on the shoulder from behind. "Meredith Nicholls?"

She turned around and found herself staring into a pair of blue-gray eyes. It was the owner of the shop that Spartacus had broken into. The man who had been sitting with his friends laughing at her.

She folded her arms. "Yes."

"So, you're the marketing expert from Boston?"

The way he said it, she still wasn't sure if he was being condescending. "Yes."

He put out his hand, offering her a handshake, and when she blatantly refused to take it, he withdrew it and ran his hand through his hair instead. "Have I offended you in any way?"

"I'm not sure." An image of him smirking with his friends refused to leave her mind. She looked over to see where Chloe had gone. Her daughter was at the other end of the refreshment tables, hovering near the cookies.

"Well, if you're not sure, then I obviously must have. I'm Dylan Fraser," he said, "Nice to meet you." He offered her his hand again, and this time, she took it.

"Enchanted," she replied. "You might be relieved to know that we didn't bring Spartacus with us."

"I would have known if you had. Half of these tables and chairs would have been overturned."

"You don't like my dog, do you?"

"I'm trying to make a joke, break the ice, that kind of thing," he said, shrugging, and slipping his hands into his pockets.

"There you are!" cried Hyacinth, before Merry had a chance to reply.

"I see you've met Dylan. That's wonderful. I was hoping to introduce you to him, and you've already beaten me to it."

Introduce Dylan, thought Merry? *Whatever for?* Please, no. A shudder rolled over her.

"Dylan's helping us with the Christmas pageant this year."

"You make it sound as if this is a first," Merry heard Dylan mutter.

"As he has been doing every year for the past four years," said Hyacinth, smiling brightly.

"Oh," said Merry, she was anxious to leave and unsure of how to respond to that. "I should get going. Chloe hasn't eaten and it's already late."

"But you need to speak to Dylan. I told him that you would help him with his business."

"You did?" This was annoying.

Dylan watched her closely.

"He's going to be spending a lot of time directing the pageant and so—"

"Not a lot of time, Hyacinth," said Dylan, interrupting. "I don't have a lot of time for the pageant. I already told you that."

"Yes, yes, I heard you, but we all need to work together if we are to make our annual Christmas pageant a success. People flock to Starling Bay for our Christmas markets and you for one will benefit from that."

"So will other people, but I don't see you asking them to help out with the pageant."

Merry listened to the exchange with interest. This man seemed to be as irritated as she was by Hyacinth's proposal. This was supposed to be her time to recuperate, and slow down to spend quality time with Chloe and relax. What she had seen tonight, and the expectations people had of her, wasn't going to help her do any slowing down or relaxing. She blamed Hyacinth for this.

She seized her moment to escape. "I really must go, Hyacinth."

"You can, but first I have some people I want you to meet. I promised them you'd help."

Merry's lips tightened. She could see Dylan staring at her with amusement dancing in his eyes.

"You promised them?"

"It's how she works, isn't it, Hyacinth?" Dylan winked at the elderly woman and flashed Merry a cheeky grin.

"I get things done around here, young man, and you know it." She turned to Merry. "Come and find me when you're done with Dylan."

"But what do you want me to do with him?" The words fell on deaf ears because Hyacinth rushed off like a bull getting ready for a fight, and worse, she'd left her alone with that man.

"What do you want me to do with him?" Dylan repeated, looking at her with his eyebrow raised. He seemed friendlier than the last time they'd met. Maybe it was the lure of free marketing advice that had done it.

"I was hoping to go home." She was eager to get away from all these people. The thought of returning to their cozy little home —Hyacinth's home—beckoned.

"I sense that you've been pushed into something you don't want to do." He was wearing a leather bomber jacket, and with his hands slipped nonchalantly into the front pockets of his jeans, he seemed suddenly larger and taller than she remembered.

She pulled her scarf from her coat pocket and put it around her neck, hoping he'd get the hint that she was in a hurry to leave. "It wasn't sold to me like that, coming here. I'm staying at one of Hyacinth's houses down by the bay. I didn't realize I had to work

46

for it. Not that anything is free," she added quickly, not wanting him to think she was being ungrateful.

"Hyacinth can be overbearing. She's a persuasive woman."

Merry wiped her fingers over her right eyebrow, as if it might help to relieve the tension that was starting to build up in her head. When things got too much, she often ended up with a dull headache. She was desperate to leave. Maybe she could put this guy off until the next time? But just as she was about to make an excuse and leave, he said, "That was a good speech."

And now she knew he was lying.

"I assumed you guys found it funny," she said, not wanting to let that go. "I saw you laughing at me with your friends."

"I wasn't laughing at you."

"I saw you." He was such a blatant liar.

"I was not laughing at you," he insisted.

She didn't believe him. He'd lie and say anything just to get an hour-long consultation out of her, like the others, but she stayed silent.

"You were good," he said, nodding his head. "I kind of sensed that Hyacinth sprang that on you."

Merry nodded. "She did. I had no idea that I'd have to stand up and make a speech, let alone spend so long talking to people afterwards."

"You did well. The audience was hanging onto your every word."

She was convinced that he was only saying this because he was trying to sweeten her. He seemed less defensive and more humble. "I can give you five minutes of my time." She made a show of looking at her watch.

"Hey, it's not a problem. We can pick this up another time. I can see you want to go home." He shrugged those incredibly wide shoulders.

"I can talk to you now," she insisted, especially since she

47

could see Chloe checking out the noticeboard at the back. "I've got a few minutes."

"I don't want to stress you out. Don't worry about it." He started to walk away.

Now she felt bad. "I'm not stressed."

"You said yourself you'd been bamboozled into doing this. I don't really need marketing help, as such. It was just Hyacinth's way of trying to get me to do the Christmas pageant."

"And you're doing it?"

"Yes," he replied, making a face. "Just as you're doing this. Getting up on stage and talking about what you do. That's typical of Hyacinth to do something like that."

"She's my mom's friend."

"Then I hate to think what your mom's enemies must be like." He smiled, revealing perfectly white teeth. It almost made her smile. He had a dimple in his chin. The tiny indentation was made more pronounced when his lips curved up, as they did now. She cleared her throat again. "Hyacinth says you've been running the pageant for a number of years. It should be easy then, shouldn't it?"

"It's hardly an epic production; twenty or so kids, and a handful of their moms helping out with the costume and props."

She was just about to say something when she heard "Mom!" She turned around at the sound of Chloe's voice. "Guess what?"

"What?"

"I signed up."

"For what?"

"The pageant."

This was news. "You did?"

Chloe nodded.

"Cool," said Dylan. Chloe glanced at him. "I'm directing the production. Dylan Fraser," he held out his hand. "Pleased to meet you."

48

"Chloe." Her daughter shook Dylan's hand. "But I don't want to act."

"You don't?" Merry and Dylan said at the same time, then looked at one another for a prolonged second.

"Then what would you like to do?" Dylan asked, scratching his chin as if he was thinking.

Chloe shrugged. "I dunno. Maybe stuff backstage."

"You mean like props, and lighting, and stagecraft?"

"I guess."

"I have a couple of helpers already, but I definitely could do with some more help on that."

Chloe's face brightened.

He pulled out something from his jacket and handed it to Merry. "I'm giving your mom my business card. Auditions start next week."

"What do I need your business card for?"

"In case Chloe has any questions," he replied easily. "But all you need to know is that we have three weeks to go, and two rehearsals a week, and the performance is in the town square on Christmas Eve. It's not a Hollywood production by any means. Things can and will go wrong, but..." he put his hands on his hips and looked around. "It works and the kids have fun, which I suppose is what it's all about."

"Is that okay, Mom?" Chloe asked. "For me to go?"

"Yes, of course it's okay." Chloe had signed up. She was interested in something for a change. Of course it was fine.

"Are you sure?" Chloe persisted.

"Is there a problem?" Dylan asked. "If you're worried about your daughter missing out on school or anything, don't be. It's in the evening. From 7:00 until 8:00."

"She's not at sch—"

"My mom hates Christmas," Chloe announced, flatly.

"Oh."

49

That was all he said, and she wondered what he was thinking. But for some reason, he didn't say what she'd been expecting. "Not at school, huh? I guess you're only here for a while so it makes sense not to start someplace new."

"We're going home after the holidays," Merry told him.

"Well, you have my card, if you have any questions about the pageant." He looked at Chloe. "It's such a low-key event, but I hope you'll have fun. You'll get to know the other kids. Oh, before I forget. Your dog-bowl is ready. Come by whenever you want to pick it up."

"Great, thanks."

Merry was about to offer her marketing help again, but he didn't seem interested, and before she could open her mouth, he'd walked off.

CHAPTER 9

a few nights later Rourke coerced Dylan and Reed into having a drink at the Blue Velvet Bar at The Grand Hotel seeing that they had missed out on their regular get together due to the meeting at the town hall.

The Grand Hotel was Starling Bay's oldest and grandest hotel, and it was where Dylan and his friends tried to meet regularly. Rourke liked to hang out here because he could watch the wave of new female visitors to the bay. The town had a couple of small cozy inns further away, but The Grand Hotel was famous and central, and it was where most of the visitors flocked. It was always busy and for Rourke—a man who never wasted an opportunity to fish in the pool that was the most full—it was ideal.

As for himself, Dylan liked to relax and get away from the workshop. Clearwater Village was quiet, and he wasn't overly friendly with many of the people there. It was a simple 'hi' and 'bye' with the other store owners and artists there. He never opened up to anyone much, but enjoyed meeting his friends.

Rourke was already waiting at the bar, which didn't surprise

Dylan. Rourke was usually the first one out of them to get there. They shared a beer and caught up on things as they waited for Reed.

"This is an honor," Rourke announced, when Reed joined them almost an hour late.

"I'm a busy man." Reed dismissed the comment with a shake of his head. Dylan noticed that he seemed wound up. "How's Olivia?"

"In New York," Reed replied, sitting down.

"Another modeling shoot?" Reed's fiancée had been Miss Wisconsin over a decade ago, and seemed to jet off frequently to modeling shoots, at least, that's what Reed had said at first, but lately he wasn't saying much and seemed grumpy each time they met.

"Who knows what she does?" Reed answered, and Dylan and Rourke looked at one another, their eyes widening. "I don't want to talk about it."

"Then let's order," Rourke suggested. They called over a server and ordered a round of drinks.

"Have you had your Marketing 101 with the 'expert from Boston' yet?" Rourke asked.

"No." He should have known Rourke would have something to say about the other night. His friends had made a quick getaway while he'd been talking to Meredith Nicholls. Rourke had winked at him and given him a thumbs-up behind her back.

"No?" Reed joined in.

"No," Dylan repeated.

"Or did she invite you back to her place that night for a more in-depth conversation?" Rourke asked. There was a mischievous glint in his eyes and Dylan knew exactly where his friend's one-track mind was heading. Something in Dylan's gut tightened. This guy had dated a fair percentage of the female population of

Starling Bay. The idea that Rourke might have an interest in Meredith Nicholls didn't sit well with him for some reason.

"No, she did not," he replied tightly. "She has a daughter, and she's not here for long."

"She has a daughter? Is there a husband?"

"She's a widow," replied Dylan, a twinge of sympathy rolling over him.

"A widow?" Reed asked, sounding surprised.

"That's sad, definitely, but…" Rourke appeared to be choosing his words carefully, "But…uh…she's probably lonely, then, don't you think?"

Dylan hung his head in disgust. This was very Rourke-esque. Insensitive. "When are you ever going to grow up?" Five years younger than him, and just turned thirty, Rourke sometimes seemed so much younger. Reed and Rourke were both the same age, but Reed seemed so much older, and wiser, and burdened with life—whether it was because of the Knight name, and legacy, or because he had too much responsibility on his shoulders.

Or maybe even because of his upcoming wedding in the summer.

For Rourke, on the other hand, life was still a big, rollicking adventure. He had no commitments, no worries, no stress.

"Her daughter's signed up to do the Christmas pageant," said Dylan, eager to deflect the talk away from the widow.

Rourke almost spat out his beer. "What? Why?"

"This is going to be interesting," said Reed, rubbing his hands together. "I wonder what Leah Shriver will make of that."

"Damnit." Dylan took a large gulp from his beer bottle. That was as big a reason as any for him not to want to do the Christmas pageant. The reason these two were killing themselves laughing was because Leah Shriver was crazy about him and he didn't feel anything towards her at all. She'd been a single mom as long as he'd known her, and she was very much interested in him.

Except that he hadn't heard from her. Usually, she would have bugged him with emails and phone calls about unimportant things relating to the pageant. "She might have moved," he told them, "I haven't heard from her in a while."

"She's waiting it out. She'll turn up at rehearsal time, just you wait and see."

It wasn't Leah Shriver he was waiting with bated breath to see or not, it was Meredith Nicholls. She hadn't told him why she hated Christmas, but he knew the reason why.

"So when are you meeting with this Meredith woman?" Reed asked. "You can't knock a free marketing consultation."

"Why are you so interested?" Dylan asked, irritated by both of his friends' sudden obsession with Meredith Nicholls.

"I need to talk business with her. If she can work wonders for you, I'm curious to see what she can do for me."

His insides tightened at the sound of that. He already knew Meredith felt put upon, judging by the conversation that had taken place between her and Hyacinth that night. It was for that same reason that he hadn't accepted her begrudging offer of help. He was certain that she wouldn't take too kindly to his friend Reed asking for some free advice.

"Take it from me," Dylan replied. "She's really busy, and I doubt she'll have time. She's not going to be here for that long."

As he recalled, she hadn't looked too happy that night. He felt sorry for her and her daughter. Poor kid. She looked like she wanted to be any place but at the town hall that night. It was probably a good thing she'd signed up for the pageant.

The next day, after doing a full day at the store, he drove to Starling Bay and arrived at the Fitzsimmons Theater, a large complex next to the town hall which was used for shows and performances, mainly during the summer. It had a dance studio as well, but Dylan used the stage in the main theater for the rehearsals, even though the actual performance would take place outside in the town square.

Armed with the same old script from previous years, he walked in. He could see some moms and children already waiting around the stage area. He greeted them with a cheeriness he didn't feel, and was eager to get the night over and done with.

"Good evening, all," he said, raising his voice so that they could hear him. "Nice to see so many of you here today. Please don't be nervous about the performance. Some of you will be familiar with it, but for some of you, it will be a new experience." A sea of faces stared back at him. There were many new faces, but Meredith Nicholls and her daughter were nowhere to be seen. He hoped Chloe hadn't changed her mind and chickened out. In the same breath he realized that Leah Shriver and her son weren't here either, but this was a matter for celebration, not disappointment.

He chatted briefly with the moms, answering their questions, and reassuring them that the performance always went smoothly, and there was no need to worry. It was odd that he had to reassure the parents, and not the children.

"Yes, twice a week," he said to a new mom who asked him about the frequency of the rehearsals. "But we might have a few extra ones as we get to the week of the performance."

Just then he noticed that Meredith and Chloe had turned up. They were walking down the aisle, peering towards the front of the stage, looking a little lost. The other parents stood around in groups while their children played and talked with one another. It was probably bewildering to Meredith and her daughter, not knowing anyone.

He walked up to them, smiling, and wanting to reassure them. Chloe appeared a little anxious. "Hey," he said, giving her an I'm-sorry-I-laughed-at-you smile. "You made it."

"She couldn't wait to get out of the house," Meredith told him.

"Homeschooling sucks."

"Chloe!"

"It does, Mom."

"It's not *proper* homeschooling. I only gave you a few math problems."

"Math is good to know," he said. But Chloe wasn't paying attention. She was staring in the direction of the stage. "That's a big stage."

"We're not doing the performance here," he explained. "You probably don't know but the final performance will be outside in one corner of the town square."

"Outside?" Meredith asked, looking worried.

"That sounds awesome!" Chloe cried.

"Are you sure you don't want a part in the play?"

"I'm sure. I just want to help out."

"That's fine." There wasn't that much to do, the costumes were taken care of. They used the same ones every year, and Leah was in charge of those. But he was sure he could find something that would keep Chloe busy and make her feel that she was part of this. Ordinarily, he wouldn't pander to any child's needs, but somehow he couldn't bring himself to say that to Chloe, and he didn't know why that was.

"We have one rehearsal a week," he said, "and then maybe an extra one or two in the week of the performance."

"When's that?"

"Christmas Eve."

"You don't have long to go," Meredith pointed out.

"I am well aware of that."

She was silent for a few moments, then, "I'm sorry about the other day." He blinked at her in surprise, the apology being so unexpected. "The other day?" he asked, noticing that she had nice eyes; soft eyes, but they were touched by sadness.

"At the town hall, regarding the marketing advice I'm supposed to be giving you and everyone else." She pulled off her mustard-colored woolen hat and ran her hands through her silky soft hair.

"Hyacinth can be demanding and obnoxious," he stated. "And she's used to getting her own way."

"Yes, she can. I see that now."

They smiled at one another, this shared opinion melting some of the coldness that had lingered between them from their previous meeting.

"Don't worry too much about the marketing advice. I can see you have a lot going on. I'm sure Hyacinth had a lot of people lined up for you to talk to."

"She did."

He'd hung around long after the two of them had stopped talking, and had ended up staying on at the Town Hall anyway because he'd met a couple of the other business owners he was friendly with. Like him, Meredith had also been there until the very end.

"Chloe mentioned you're not too fond of Christmas…" He watched her reaction, hoping that she would tell him something about herself. Her face softened, and he sensed a sadness, more than anything.

"It used to be fun, once upon a time."

"But not so now?" he asked, his voice soft. He didn't want to pry, yet he couldn't help but ask the question. She opened her mouth to say something, then hesitated.

"You don't have to answer if you don't feel comfortable. It's not my place to ask."

"Aren't we supposed to be starting?" A voice behind him interrupted them and his insides hardened. He could recognize that grating voice anywhere. He didn't even have to turn his head because Leah Shriver planted herself squarely between them.

"Hello, Leah."

"Dylan." The woman kissed him on the cheek. "It's been a long time. How have you been?"

"The same as I was last month when I saw you at the store, Leah," he replied, calmly.

"It seems like a long time ago," she twittered, then turned to Meredith. "I'm Leah Shriver," she said, holding out her hand.

"I'm Meredith, but most people call me Merry."

"Merry?" he asked.

"As in *Merry* Christmas?" Leah asked.

Meredith's smile faded.

My mom hates Christmas. Chloe's remark came back to him.

"When did you move here?" Leah asked, missing the cue, the downcast expression on Merry's face. He'd noticed.

"I'm...I'm not staying. I'm only here for a while."

"We should get together," Leah said to Merry. "We'll go and get a cup of coffee one morning. I'll tell you who's who and what's what around here."

He could read Merry's face and saw the disappointment all over it.

"I'm—I'm—I don't have a lot of free time," Merry said, forcing a laugh out of herself. Leah had cornered her, the way only Leah knew how to. He had to rescue her.

"Excuse me, ladies," he said, stepping away and clapping his hands together. "Parents, if you don't mind, I'd like you to leave now so that we can get on with the show." He beamed for effect, then remembered. "Please come back promptly at eight to pick up your children."

No matter how many times he said it, there were still parents who turned up ten or sometimes fifteen minutes late. It was rude, and it ate into his evening, and he was a busy man. After the rehearsal he still had to go back to his workshop and work on the vases.

CHAPTER 10

$\mathcal{I}$t had been jarring, the way Leah Shriver had rudely interrupted her and Dylan, and her suggestion that they both get to know one another over coffee made Merry shudder.

Up until then she had been enjoying a pleasant conversation with the quiet, but not-so-bad-looking store owner. He seemed easy to talk to, and she wasn't sure why she suddenly found herself in a conversation with someone she barely knew. It wasn't the type of thing she did. If anything, she had closed herself off in the last few years, preferring to concentrate on work, and getting through each day.

Advice from her parents and friends, to 'go out there and have fun' had fallen on deaf ears. Fun? Life was never going to be fun again.

As the rehearsal started, she saw most of the moms leave, and was tempted to sit a few rows back, along the side nearest the wall. She planned to catch up with emails and messages to friends who wanted to know how she was settling in Starling Bay.

Now that she was no longer tethered to work, and wasn't in a rush to meet deadlines or attend meetings, she wasn't at her phone's beck and call, and didn't check it as much.

She didn't watch TV much either.

Ever since they had arrived here, she had spent most of her free time reading, and daydreaming. She and Chloe often took Spartacus for long walks, and explored the town. It was a luxury that was new to her, a world away from her working day, and she was getting to like it.

As she sat down, going through the messages on her phone, she looked up to see that Leah had seen her. Dylan had mentioned that she helped with costumes and props, but Merry also detected something between this woman and Dylan.

It was just a gut feeling, and she had nothing concrete to substantiate her claim. The woman smiled at her, and Merry grew more worried. The last thing she wanted was for Leah Shriver to come and talk to her again.

She decided to leave. She didn't want to sit here in fear of Leah pouncing on her. Once outside, she headed away from the theater, and towards the oceanfront. She couldn't see the water. In the darkness it was a blanket of silky black, a floating pane of glass that reflected the lights off the lamps. It was colder here, and the wind swept off the water and chilled her bones.

She had been so hasty to leave that she wasn't even sure where she was going, so she just walked along the bay, past the big hotel. For a moment she was tempted to go inside. The warm lights welcomed her, but she knew nobody in this place, and the thought of wandering into a fancy hotel like that on her own put her off the idea so she carried on walking; after all, the idea was to get away and have some downtime—away from the busy city, away from work, away from the memories that swirled around her like mist on the sea.

After Brian's death she had thrown herself into her work, but had she moved on? She wasn't sure. And she had neglected Chloe. Not neglected her welfare, for her daughter had the best of anything that money could buy, but she hadn't been there for her as much as she should have been. It was only because her parents had cushioned the blow of their loss, and had been around to take care of them, that she and Chloe had survived and were able to slowly heal and move on.

She continued to walk and soon came upon what looked like a small, cozy café. The owner had decorated it beautifully. The windows were bedecked in fairy lights, and as she peeked through the windows, she saw a Christmas tree next to the point of sale counter. Red, gold and green tinsel draped prettily from the walls.

It was inviting. She looked up to read the name of the place.

Roxy's Diner.

She liked the sound of that; cute and cozy. Warm air kissed her skin as soon as she stepped inside. The place was three-quarters full, but she didn't feel self-conscious walking in here alone. Her cold face suddenly warmed up. This seemed like the perfect place to pass the time.

Taking a seat near the window, she admired the shimmering fairy lights, and when a server appeared, ordered a cup of hot chocolate. Then she got out her book and lost herself in it.

It was only when her cell phone rang much later on, that Merry looked up. She grabbed her phone to answer it and saw the time.

Goodness! It was twenty minutes past eight. She was late. Then she grew fearful because it was a number she didn't recognize. She answered it quickly.

"Mom!" cried Chloe. "You're late! Where are you?"

"Sorry!" she gasped, grabbing her bag, her book and her coat. "I'm coming!" She tore out of Roxy's Diner and tried to run all the way back along the bay. But this time the distance stretched out in the cold chill of the inky night. She had to stop every few seconds to catch her breath.

How had she not realized? She would normally set an alarm—at least, the *highly-organized Meredith* would. She'd just become a little less organized, a little less time-conscious. She paused for breath near The Grand Hotel, relieved that the theater was only a few minutes from here.

Chloe sounded mad at her, but it was Dylan she was worried about. The man had made it a point to tell parents not to be late and she had failed on the first attempt. Her cell phone rang again, and she quickly fished it out of her bag, saw that it was the same number as before, and didn't answer it.

"I'm coming!" she hissed angrily, more to herself than anyone else, and made a concerted effort to run, even if it killed her.

At last, breathless and disorientated, as if she'd climbed a huge mountain, she flew through the main theater doors. In the center of the lobby stood Chloe with Dylan, and a couple of other people were over by the vending machine. She felt relieved. She couldn't have been that late if there were other parents around.

Feeling uplifted, she rushed towards her daughter and gave her a bear hug. "Sorry!" she cried, kissing the top of Chloe's head, an outpouring of relief rolling over her.

"Mom!" Chloe shrugged out of her embrace. "You're cold."

"I...know..." she said, breathing hard as if the oxygen levels in the air suddenly dropped. She tried in vain to catch her breath, then turned to Dylan. "I'm *so* sorry. I ..." she took a few breaths ... "I know you warned us all, but I lost track of time—"

Dylan put out his hand, halting her. "Stop. Take it easy and catch your breath. It's okay."

She tried to still her breathing. "I shouldn't have kept you waiting. I'm sorry."

"It's okay."

Her face was probably tomato-red and she must have looked a sight. When was the last time she'd ever had to run for anything? She drove everywhere, or caught an Uber. She'd never had to run for *anything*. She fanned her face, feeling the heat rising to her cheeks. "I'm so out of shape," she confessed.

"You don't look out of shape." Dylan's gaze didn't lower to the rest of her body, he kept it level, but her cheeks heated up some more. "I mean," he shrugged, as if he'd realized he'd said something he shouldn't have but didn't care about it. "You *don't*."

Him saying that sent a shiver all over her. It was a feeling she hadn't experienced in a long, long time.

She opened her mouth, to pooh-pah his comment, but didn't want to seem as if she was inviting him to pay her more compliments, even though this felt nice. This man was saying nice things to her. Not just that, he was paying some attention to her. Goodness. It really had been a while since she'd spoken to a man who wasn't a boyfriend of a friend or a work colleague.

They stared at one another, and she tried to figure out what this was. An awkward pause, or a *moment*. Because her heart was beating like crazy.

She noticed that he was wearing that leather bomber jacket again, and she was either ovulating and her hormones had gone crazy, or she was coming down with something, because her gaze settled on the man for a couple of seconds longer than it should have.

"We should go," she said, turning to her daughter. "Why didn't you call me from your phone?"

"Because my battery died," Chloe replied. "Were you doing your work emails again?"

"No. I was reading, and I got carried away." She pulled her hat down over her ears, noting that they suddenly felt cold.

"Reading?" Chloe shrieked. "Mom, you were so late."

"It's okay, Chloe," Dylan said.

"I can't be that late if there are still some people around." Merry glanced over his shoulder and nodded at the people by the vending machine. It was Leah Shriver and her son.

"Peter and his mom were waiting with Dylan," said Chloe, in a how-could-you-do-this-to-me tone.

64

"Oh." Dots were trying to connect in her brain, but a fog suddenly settled. *Was Leah with Dylan? Were they an item?*

"Leah Shriver's a busybody," Dylan explained, and looked away, unable to meet her gaze when he said it.

"Mom, can I get some money for the machine?"

Merry took out some coins and handed them to her then watched Chloe walk away. A bittersweet twinge of *something* stabbed her. She wasn't exactly sure what, or why. She glossed over this recent revelation and adopted a nonchalant tone. "I was going to say, I'd be happy to look over your marketing materials and offer you any advice, seeing that I owe you."

Dylan shook his head. "I don't want to put you out, and you don't owe me."

"I've made you late." Whatever his plans were for tonight, she'd kept him waiting.

"I'm not going anywhere. You haven't put me out."

She wondered if that nugget of information had been for her benefit, and if it had been deliberate. Or maybe she was reading too much into it?

"Nevertheless, I like to pay my dues. Hyacinth wants me to, and Chloe seems to like coming here otherwise she wouldn't be so angry at me for being late. It's the least I can do."

"Are you sure?"

"I'm sure. Plus, I'd rather not explain to Hyacinth why I haven't had my consultation with you."

"She does keep track."

She could see Chloe walking back. "Call me when you're free. You have my number."

"I do, and I will."

CHAPTER 11

A bell tinkled as she opened the door, but when she stepped inside, there was no one around. It was early though, just after nine, but the door had been open so she assumed Dylan would be here, especially since he'd called her and arranged for her to come this morning.

She walked around, looking at the different displays, and saw that display table which Spartacus had trashed was now restored.

Large coffee mugs in pretty colors and with gorgeous designs were on display. Some had quotes written over with Starling Bay and its various landmarks, painted in. She was impressed by the intricate art work.

"Oh, hey." His voice made her jump. She spun around, caught off guard by his sudden appearance. "Sorry, I didn't mean to frighten you."

"It's…it's all right." He was in his work clothes, for his shirt was dirty with paint and dried clay marks, and he'd rolled his sleeves up to his elbows. She looked away. It was easier to look at the objects on display than to face him. The sight of those nicely muscled, bare arms was doing peculiar things to her breathing again.

"I always open first thing in the morning, but we don't get any visitors until after 11:00."

"I'm early, then?"

"No." He wiped his hands on a cloth. "It's better you came now, when it's quieter."

"I must have interrupted you. You look like the quintessential artist."

"I was making some vases in the back."

"Vases?"

"In my workshop."

"You have a workshop, and you make all of these things?" This was impressive.

He laughed. "Most of them. The ones I've made will say 'handmade' on it. Which reminds me," he walked away to one of the display cupboards. "You didn't come by for your dog-bowl." He pulled out a large red dog bowl with *Spartacus* painted across it.

"Wow. That's gorgeous, and so beautifully painted. Thank you." She didn't have him down for someone who made things out of clay, much less painted them as well, and he was doing that on top of the Christmas pageant.

"I'm glad you like it. I hope your dog likes it too."

"If it has food in it, he will."

She looked around at the items on display, seeing everything with new eyes, then picked up one of the large coffee cups and saw the 'handmade' label underneath. "You painted this?" She held up the sky blue cup with its picture of Starling Bay and a pretty line of shops and buildings along the bay front and an aquamarine sea.

He nodded.

"It's beautiful. Absolutely beautiful."

"Thank you."

"You do this all day long?"

"Yes."

"It's…gorgeous, such stunning attention to detail. I never assumed you were so creative. I thought you were just a shop owner…" She stopped, realizing that her comment sounded rude. "Sorry, not *just* a shop owner but…but…" She was in awe, a little *too much*, and she needed to rein it in. Only, the cups were gorgeous, and as she walked around and admired the rest of his wares, she was even more amazed by the intricacy of his designs. "You're talented," she said, casting her eye over a display of vases. "I could *never* do anything like this."

He laughed. "Have you ever tried?"

"No."

"When you spend a lot of time doing something, you naturally get better at it. I spend half the day in the workshop, and the rest of it in the store. I can't always keep up with the production, especially around Christmastime, but I try to make as many of these things as I can. I sell some of them in one of the other gift shops by the bay. It's not mine, but it helps to have my products in as many places as I can."

"Smart move." She was definitely impressed. Her assumption that he was just a store owner was clearly wrong. Running a store was hard enough, but to make and sell the goods as well, she could only guess at the time constraints and stress of managing a business like that. "It must take time, making these."

He nodded. "It does. It takes up a lot of my time, but it's what I love to do, so it doesn't really feel like work."

"You're a lucky man. Not many people can say that about their line of work."

"I'm good with my hands."

She glanced at them, and a shiver shocked over her skin as he said it. Those hands, big, and strong… She shook her head, trying to displace the thought that had sprung up from nowhere; a thought of him with his hands around her waist.

"We're all good at something," he said, placing the dirty rag over his shoulder and folding his arms. She looked away to stop her gaze from falling on those naked forearms.

Forcing herself to move away, she turned her back to him because this close proximity to Dylan Fraser was definitely not good for her.

"I couldn't do something like this." She nodded at a display. "I was never creative. Chloe gets it from—" She stopped herself. It didn't seem right to talk about Brian.

"You're the marketing expert," said Dylan, smoothly. "You're obviously good at something. I can never wrap my head around that stuff and if I had my way, I'd carry on making things and not worry about the marketing side of the business. I'd probably be doing a whole lot better if I had your brains."

"I doubt it." She didn't see it like that. She hadn't gone to college, and had no degree to her name. Her job had been a natural progression. She and Brian had married young and had Chloe within the same year. They had been idealistic dreamers. Instead of worrying about how they were going to bring Chloe up, they'd just gone with the flow and things had worked out. They had worked hard. Back then they hadn't had fancy cars or a plush apartment, but they hadn't needed that.

She had proven herself as a salesclerk at Boyd & Meyer, and had absorbed everything around her; things on the store floor, working with customers, and picking up morsels of information from the managers she worked for.

She'd ended up working around the entire store, being in different departments, and she had worked her way up. Things had started to go amazingly well for her a few years after Chloe was born. She worked harder and got promoted, and Brian was doing well at his job. They were comfortable, and happy.

But after his passing, she had worked harder than ever, had gotten a big promotion a couple of years later, but life was somehow emptier. The nice Jeep and fancy apartment didn't mean much anymore. She would have given anything to have had that small home with Brian from back when they had first gotten married.

"Hyacinth has been blowing your trumpet. Even my friends are interested in meeting you, but don't worry, I told them you were busy and had no time left. I'd much rather have you to myself. I mean, not in that capacity, obviously."

Once again she felt the color trickling to her cheeks, and she wished she would stop taking everything he said literally.

"Hyacinth is an old friend of my mother's," she said, picking up a vase and examining it. It was easier to concentrate on the vase when Dylan said things like that. "She's just being nice."

"You're a marketing manager for a big department store in Boston. You must be doing something right."

"Let's see if we can do something right for you," she said. "You have beautiful products. Starling Bay is an affluent town, and it's a tourist haven. We should be able to do something to increase your footfall."

"I was hoping to increase my profits."

"More footfall should theoretically lead to more profits, and when it comes to profit, hope isn't a good tactic."

He smiled. "I like that."

"It's true."

"I have an office at the back where we can talk."

"But," she glanced at the door. "What if customers arrive?"

"Laura will be in soon, but I have a bell on the door and I can hear it in the office. And I'm not expecting a beast like Spartacus to come charging through the door again. How is he?"

"My beast?" she asked, amused. "He's feeling cooped up. The house is way too small for him."

"You need a mansion," he replied dryly. There it was again, his smile, warm and easy. She wasn't one to notice smiles much, or people, or have conversations with strangers—and Dylan Fraser was a stranger.

Also, there was a good chance that he and Leah Shriver were an item.

As it was, she found she was more relaxed and at ease these days, and she noticed such things. Or maybe she noticed these things on him more? Taking time out from work had been a good thing. Being in Starling Bay had been a good thing.

"I need to get changed," he announced, looking down at his shirt and filling her mind with an image of him shirtless. She swallowed, unable to find her voice.

"Follow me," he ordered, turning to leave.

"To see you get changed?" she spluttered. He'd caught her so off guard that the words whizzed right out of her mouth. She usually had a good filter for these things, she usually thought about what she was going to say before she said it, but around this man her filter turned wonky.

"What?" he glanced over his shoulder, his lips curved upwards in a questioning smile. "No...I meant if you follow me, I will show you to my office."

She felt like an idiot, and couldn't think of anything to say that would rescue her from this embarrassment.

"It's small." He opened the door to a tiny room with a desk, a computer and a chair. "I'll grab another chair."

"I'll wait here." She couldn't bring herself to look at him, and instead, shuffled into the room, then sat down on his chair.

When he left, she face palmed.

To see you get changed?

What a thing to say.

CHAPTER 12

*D*ylan wandered off into his living area to change into a fresh shirt. This large room across from the office had a kitchen area in one corner, with a sink, electric kettle, toaster and a microwave for his food.

In the other area he had a sofa, a table and a couple of chairs. He had been lucky to have a large plot for his store. Not all of the units were as big around here. He needed the space for the workshop.

But unless he found a way to get more people into his store, he was going to have to find something else to do to bring in more money. It had crossed his mind that if things didn't improve, he would need to get a job, and run his store on the side. He'd need to downsize, which meant he'd need a similar setup somewhere else, but a smaller workshop wouldn't solve things either. Being an artist did not pay the rent easily.

He should have learned that lesson from his failed days in LA, where the only jobs he'd managed to land were the hunky DIY man in a couple of low-budget soap operas.

He sprayed some cologne on because he didn't want Meredith

to smell clay on him. Then he whipped a t-shirt out of his bag and put it on.

Ten minutes later, he returned to the office and dragged in an extra chair. Meredith was sitting in his chair. This was awkward. The great big old bulky monitor had a stiff screen which wouldn't turn so he would either have to sit bunched up close to her, or sit across the desk from her. "Where do you want me?" he asked, not wanting to invade her personal space.

She looked startled. "Uh…well…"

"I'm sorry this is so cramped." He didn't want to sit so close to her because he could sense her wariness. He barely knew her, but he could tell that Meredith wasn't a woman who flirted wantonly.

Heck, she didn't flirt at all.

She was on the complete opposite end of the spectrum to Leah Shriver. And he found it refreshing—this return to innocence. He'd experienced what an absence of innocence was like, when he'd foolishly agreed to go on one of those dating sites that Rourke had pushed him into trying.

"You don't have to be sorry. I guess you wanted a larger area for your workshop. I mean, that would make sense. I can move over," she offered, "or maybe it would be better if you sat here. That would make more sense, I think, don't you? That way you can show me your marketing materials."

"Like what?" he asked. He'd been dreading this. And while he had no idea what she'd have to teach him, he didn't really have anything worthwhile to show her, not on the computer, unless she wanted to see his Word document and his pathetic attempts at the fliers he'd designed for handing out at summer craft shows. He felt inferior, and stupid, and thick, and he didn't want Meredith to think these things of him, because *this* wasn't who he was. Yet this woman made him feel as if he wasn't up to scratch. And it wasn't even her fault that he felt like this.

"Like…" she seemed to hesitate, seemed unsure.

"Just say it," he prompted. "I'm not good at figures, and I'm not good at spreading the word about the business. I'm lousy at it, if you must know. What kind of stuff did you want to look at?"

"Your advertising campaigns," she suggested. "Any social media stuff?"

No way. "I don't have any of those. I hate that stuff."

She gave a chuckle. "I hate social media, too," she said, her voice soft, and smooth, and non-judgmental. Yet he felt silly, as if he'd flunked a test at school. He folded his arms.

"These *advertising* campaigns, how easy are they to set up?" He'd read about those things, and had dabbled, as in spent less than a minute trying to figure it out, but had given up. His method for spreading the word about his store was to place ads in the local papers, going so far as nearby towns, and having fliers in this shop. That was about it.

"They can be tricky—"

"Coffee?" he asked, saying it at the same time that she spoke. "I'm sorry, go on." This was uncomfortable for him and he was looking for a distraction.

"I was going to say that the ads can be tricky, if you don't know what you're doing, but I can show you. And, although you say you hate social media on a personal level, I would say that it's crucial for business. People don't read newspapers to find out what's going on, especially when it comes to products they're interested in buying, they go online, and that's where *you* need to be. Coffee would be a good idea," she said, smiling.

And at that kind of offer, and with that type of smile, his defenses loosened, and he nodded. "Coffee it is," he said. "Follow me."

He showed her into his living area. "It's not much, and you'll have to excuse the mess."

"It's *fine*," she said, sitting down at the table as he busied

74

himself making coffee. "You don't have to keep apologizing. You have a lovely store, and I'm sorry my dog crashed into it that first time."

He pulled out two cups, then turned around, waiting for the water to boil, and with no chair to sit at, remained standing. "It's okay," he replied, and he didn't really feel sorry about that any more. He was grateful that Spartacus and his owner had suddenly appeared in his life. "Thanks for coming out here."

"Out here?" She looked surprised. "You make it sound as if it's miles from civilization. It's only a short drive from town."

"But it is out of the way. It's not exactly central to town which is where it would make sense for me to be, but the rents are high there, and this is ideal for someone like me. I prefer my own space. It's nice around here, out of the way."

"Clearwater Village," Meredith said. "It has a nice ring to it."

He hadn't thought about the name much. "It's named after the lake."

"I know. I saw it in the brochure."

"It's at the other end of the forest."

"I saw there was an astrology shop a few doors down."

He rolled his eyes. "That's a new addition. But I think it's helping my store."

"Really?" she asked, surprised.

"People seem to come out of there feeling all happy, seems like they're in a good buying mood. It must be all that made-up stuff she tells them."

"Made-up stuff?"

"Surely you don't believe that mumbo-jumbo?" he asked, incredulous.

"I wouldn't knock it."

"You think people's lives are dictated by the sun and the stars?"

"I like to think we're all connected."

"But what do the sun and the stars have to do with that?"

"We're part of a wider cosmos, everything's interrelated."

"I don't buy into that."

"With you being an artist I wouldn't have thought you'd dismiss this stuff so easily."

"I'm a pragmatic man, besides, with you being a numbers woman, I wouldn't have thought you'd be into this stuff."

The kettle whistled just then and he turned around and made the coffee, but an alarm sounded on his cell phone at the same time.

"Oh, shoot," he said, turning to face her.

"What's wrong?"

"I'm supposed to be meeting with the bank manager." He stared at his phone wondering if he had time to cancel the meeting which was in less than an hour. Probably not. He'd already canceled the first meeting, and he needed this loan just so that he could pay his taxes.

"Right now?"

"Soon. I'm really sorry. I can't cancel this one."

"It's okay," said Meredith. "These things happen, and I'd hate for you to miss your meeting with someone as important as your bank manager."

"It's just that it's the second time. I missed the first one because I was making some vases, and I lost track of time. It happens when I'm on the pottery wheel."

"A pottery wheel?" she asked, sounding interested.

"It's where I shape clay, into different things, like vases, and cups, and dog bowls."

"They always look like fun. Making something 'grow' out of a slab of clay."

"I can show you quickly if you want."

"Another time," she said, getting up. "We can schedule our meeting to another day. You just let me know and I'll come back."

"Are you sure?" He warmed to the prospect of her coming back. "I'm free tomorrow, if you are."

"Tomorrow is good for me."

It wasn't looking like such a bad day, after all. "Thanks."

"I left my bag in your office," she said, heading back there to retrieve it and her belongings. He decided to leave now as well, and quickly got his folder and the paperwork he'd put aside for today's bank meeting. "I'll leave now as well," he told her.

"What if you have visitors?"

He walked out into the main store again, and started to lock up. "My part-time helper will be here soon." He could tell by the look on her face that she seemed to find it strange, him locking up his shop and leaving. That kind of thing most likely never happened where she was from. But then life was probably different in Boston, more hectic, and fast-paced.

Life in Starling Bay was more laidback. Meredith Nicholls just wasn't used to it yet.

They walked towards the parking lot. "I appreciate you coming over."

"You're welcome." She climbed into her Jeep and rolled the window down. "Thanks for the coffee. I'll come by tomorrow. Any particular time?"

"Whatever works best for you."

"Same time as today then."

"Bring Chloe if you want."

"I have Hyacinth's housekeeper at my disposal. It's easier for Chloe to stay at home with Spartacus." She turned the key but the engine didn't start right away. He peered closer as she tried again. This time the Jeep started.

"Want me to take a look at that?" he asked.

"It's working now," she said, smiling. "It acts up sometimes."

"Sometimes?"

"It's acted up once or twice."

"I can take a look at it if you want."

"Thank you, but it's not a problem. This hasn't happened since I left Boston, and I'll get it checked out when I go back."

He definitely didn't like the sound of that, and his expression must have indicated that.

"I can take care of myself, Dylan," she insisted.

He liked the way his name rolled off her tongue. "Everything about you tells me you can."

"I'll come by tomorrow."

"I look forward to it."

CHAPTER 13

"*Y*ou're leaving me with the babysitter again?" Chloe's eyes blazed back at her, and she wondered how much anger a twelve-year-old was capable of.

"I thought you didn't mind being at home? You said you preferred being at home." That's what Chloe had told her the last time. "Chloe." Merry stared down at her daughter trying to figure out what was going on inside that head of hers. Chloe had Brian's features, his forehead and nose and hair color, and she reminded Merry so much of the man she had loved and lost.

Sometimes, it was like a punch in the stomach just to look at her.

"Go then," Chloe snapped. "Just go and leave me like you always do."

"I don't always leave you." Merry was going to suggest that Chloe could come along, but it would be difficult to have a meeting with her daughter there.

"You *do* leave me. You *always* left Grandma and Grandpa to take care of me." Chloe's angry eyes flashed back at her, riddled with accusation. Merry walked away, eager to get going. She had a meeting with Dylan, then a few consultations with some other people that Hyacinth had set up for her to see. She didn't want to deal with Chloe now.

But then she stopped and turned back. This was where she'd been going wrong.

"Look, Chloe." She walked back to the couch and sat beside Chloe. "Could you please turn that off?" Her daughter had turned the TV on and turned the sound up. "Chloe," she said, raising her voice. But Chloe did nothing.

The insolence of the child. Only, Chloe wasn't a child anymore. She was on the verge of becoming a teenager. "Turn that down, please, young lady." Merry's voice turned stern. But it did the trick. Chloe silenced the TV but wouldn't look at her.

"Chloe," she said, trying again. She placed her finger under her daughter's chin, trying to get her to turn her face. "I understand you're angry at me. I'm sorry. I have to go and see someone to help them with their business. How about when I come back, we'll go around the town square again and look at the Christmas lights? And then I'll take you to that nice little place where I got hot chocolate from last week."

No answer.

She took that to be a 'yes'. Small steps. She leaned forward and kissed her daughter on the cheek lightly. "I love you. I'll be back real quick, and then we'll get some nice hot chocolate. You've got a rehearsal tomorrow. Won't that be something to look forward to?"

"Only if you're not late again."

"I won't be."

As she drove to Dylan's store again, she decided to cancel with the other people she was scheduled to see. They could complain to Hyacinth all they wanted. She had a meeting with Hyacinth too, she remembered, and she was going to cancel that too. This wasn't fair.

The thought of Hyacinth made her stomach turn. The woman

was always roping her in and yesterday she'd gone to the town hall again to sit in on yet another meeting that the committee was having with regards to the Christmas pageant.

Merry didn't even have much input to that meeting, and there was nothing she could recommend this late into the month that would help them with their efforts to get more visitors to attend. If this was what it meant not having to pay rent, she would gladly have paid, instead of having to be at Hyacinth's beck and call.

"I can't stay for too long today," she said, as soon as she walked into Dylan's store and saw him by the counter. "I'm sorry, that's lame, isn't it?"

"No. I had things to do yesterday, and you obviously have a busy schedule today. So much for taking a break in Starling Bay. Coffee?" he asked, leading her towards his living area again.

"Sure."

"Good, because I haven't had my first cup of the day. I was waiting for you to show up."

"You were?" She followed him in and noticed that there were a couple more chairs at the table today. They stared at one another across the table, him standing over by the countertop waiting for the kettle to boil, her standing around doing nothing.

"I'm going to cancel all my meetings after this one with you, including the one with Hyacinth."

Dylan's eyes glowed with something that looked like admiration. "I'm impressed. You're standing up to Hyacinth. It's about time somebody said 'no' to that woman."

"I feel obliged because she gave me her place to stay in."

Dylan nodded, and exhaled slowly. "You're in a difficult position."

"And she knows it."

"Good on you for standing up to her."

"I haven't canceled anything yet. I will, after my coffee."

"My day doesn't properly start until I've had coffee."

"I want to spend the day with Chloe. It's not fair to leave her at home with the babysitter again."

"How is she?" he wanted to know.

Merry paused, not sure how she was going to answer that. "She wasn't too pleased about being left at home again."

"You should have brought her here. Should have brought your beast, too."

"My dog is a liability here, remember."

"How could I forget? We have a lot of open space out here. There are a lot of fields for him to run around in."

"I'll have to remember that next time. But I wouldn't let Chloe walk the dog alone. I don't know the area well and I tend not to trust people I don't know. Not you, of course," she said quickly.

"Of course not," he returned quickly, a smirk settling across his face. "We could all go for a walk. It's pretty around here, if you like that sort of thing." He shrugged again, forcing her gaze to drop to those wide shoulders of his. It was crazy, that these thoughts, long ago buried, were suddenly surfacing every time she was near Dylan Fraser.

"Spart would love it."

"Chloe might, too. Maybe you could bring her next time," he continued.

"I will. I'll suggest that to her."

"It's not a bad thing, not being so trusting. You can't be too careful when it comes to your children."

"Do you have children?" she asked, wanting to know.

He shook his head. "I never got married, and so … no."

She sensed there was a story behind those words, and that he was holding back. So she didn't pursue her line of questioning.

The kettle boiled and he poured the coffee into the cups, then turned and asked her about milk and sugar. "I'll add mine, if you don't mind."

"Go ahead." He moved out of the way. "Would it be okay if we sat here?" he asked, moving over to the table. "It's too cramped in my dingy little office."

"Sure." She was relieved. The thought of sitting next to him in that small space was going to make her lose focus. She looked back at him and wondered how he had switched from the guy who'd annoyed the heck out of her at their first meeting, to this? And what did he mean by 'We could all go for a walk?' Why would he do that?

"Ready?" he asked, looking over at her. She grabbed her cup of coffee and walked over. He had a notebook with some scribbles on it. "What I'm after is a marketing strategy," he said, looking her squarely in the eye. "I know what I do well, and I kind of understand what you do well, so I'm thinking we could put our heads together and find a way to make it work."

A shiver rolled down her stomach again, and she took a cautious sip of her coffee, being extra careful not to slurp. And then she wondered if she had brushed her hair properly before she'd rushed out of the house. That little episode with Chloe had set her back.

"Make it work?" she asked, buying time, trying to get a handle on things even as the faint scent of Dylan's aftershave floated over to her, rendering her unable to think.

"Increase my profits," he stated. She stared at him, and wondered how old he was, for he had a manliness about him, a weathered and resistant feel, that was hard to ignore. "I'm interested to hear what you had in mind."

"What I had in mind?" she asked weakly. Could he read her mind? Did he know what she was thinking? It had been so long since she had felt like this with a man that she was no longer sure how to behave.

"What you had in mind regarding the marketing." Thank goodness he clarified. "I'm doing it all wrong, obviously. I don't

83

do much in the way of it, but the small bit I do isn't effective. That's why I'm in this mess in the first place. I need you to tell me how to fix it."

"Right," she sipped her coffee again. *Right.* Profits, and marketing, and all that other stuff. That was the reason she was here. Not to sit around admiring his features, or gazing at the span of his shoulders. Or inhaling his cologne as if it were a new supply of oxygen.

Starling Bay had changed her brain function to the point that she didn't recognize who this new Meredith was. "Okay—" She could do this. She could talk about work and metrics.

"I guess what I'm asking," he said, setting down his coffee cup slowly. "Is for you to go through the basics of how you would approach advertising. What would *you* do if you were in my shoes?"

"If I were in your shoes?" she asked, sitting back and putting her thinking hat on. "Okay, well," she pulled out her notepad and pen. "Show me your product line, and then I'll talk you through the basics."

CHAPTER 14

*I*t was rehearsal night again, and Dylan had never looked forward to rehearsals as much as he did tonight.

Things got even better as soon as he saw Meredith walk in. He headed in her direction, not wanting to waste any time. She was all dressed up, he noticed. Of course, he had also changed before coming here.

Twice.

But that had been because he'd been working on the wheel again and had clay marks all over his shirt. "We meet again."

"Yes, we do," Meredith replied. Chloe was in the corner talking to the other children. "She's made friends. Incredible."

"She likes coming here." The kid was lonely, that had been his observation after seeing her at the rehearsal last week. Technically, this wasn't a rehearsal for Chloe, since she didn't have a part in the play, but he had given her plenty of things to do. Lighting checks, costume and prop checks. A little of it was overlap with what Leah did, but that busybody made it a point to be involved in everything she could get her interfering hands on.

She'd been foisted on him by Hyacinth and he had no say in the matter, so he did what he could to stay out of her way.

"I'm glad she likes something about Starling Bay," Merry pointed out.

"She doesn't like it here?" He didn't like the sound of that, and looking at her, he would never have thought it. Not that he knew much about kids but he sensed that Chloe had some beef with her mom, and he hoped mother and daughter would be able to sort it out.

"I took her for hot chocolate yesterday, thinking it might improve her mood."

"At the hotel?"

"At the diner."

"Roxy's place?"

"That's the one. It's cozy in there. I like it."

"It's not bad."

"I like the hot chocolate there."

He didn't recall it being spectacular; he didn't go to Roxy's Diner much. "I can't say I remember trying it."

"It's good." The tone of her voice seconded her approval.

"I'll have to try it. Didn't it do the trick with Chloe?"

"She didn't like it, or the diner. I don't think she wanted to be there at all. If she could have had her way she would have been on her phone texting her friends."

"Kids," he said, with a shrug. "And cell phones. They're the new addiction."

"It's worrying."

He considered it lucky that this wasn't a problem he had to worry about. Being kid-free was a bonus as far as he was concerned, but Chloe seemed sweet, and she had been eager to help. He liked her attitude.

Over the years, he'd hired many students older than Chloe to help out in his store, and he'd seen firsthand the lazy attitude of some of them; many seemed to want to do as little as possible while still expecting to get paid.

He saw none of this in Chloe. "She's missing her friends back home?"

Meredith nodded. "I don't know why. It's not like we're staying here forever. We'll be leaving once the new year is in."

"Oh," he replied, as a trickle of disappointment came over him. There was no reason for it; he barely knew this woman, but he was getting to know her, and he liked her company. Something about her fit just right, even though he couldn't pinpoint what it was. "I should start," he announced, suddenly conscious that he had been talking to Merry for a while. He scanned around the room and could see moms looking at him, waiting for him to give the signal for them to leave.

Leah was busy behind the stage, staying out of his way, it seemed like. Meredith Nicholls being here had probably put her nose out of joint. "Are you staying?"

"Me? No. I've got to be somewhere." Her gaze drifted to something behind him, and then Chloe appeared.

"I'm going to leave now, and I promise not to be late, okay?" Merry dropped a kiss on her daughter's head. "Goodness! I'm running late as it is. Bye!"

She rushed off, and it made him curious. Curious to know where she was rushing off to, and who she was meeting. Not that it was any of his business, but the idea prickled him all the same.

"Have you checked that we have all the costumes according to that list I gave you?" he asked Chloe. She nodded. "But there was something I needed to double check," she said, and rushed off.

He clapped his hands together and told the parents to leave, and just as he was getting ready to start the rehearsal, Leah strode up to him. "Peter's a *donkey*?"

"We need a donkey."

"Why couldn't he be one of the three wise men?"

"Leah, if I gave in to all the parents' requests for their children to have main parts, there would be no play."

They stood side-by-side, facing the children who were sitting cross-legged on the floor awaiting instructions. Chloe darted across from one end of the stage to the other, and disappeared in the wings. "Why is *she* getting special treatment?" Leah hissed under her breath.

The children stared up at them. He turned to Leah. "Are you seriously asking me that?" he snapped back, keeping his voice to a whisper. The only way to block out Leah Shriver was to turn his back on her and begin. Without waiting for her reply, he stepped forward to address the waiting children. "Has everyone had a chance to go through their lines?"

A chorus of 'yeses' rang out.

"Good, then let's get started."

The only incentive to get him through the rehearsal was the chance to see Merry Nicholls at the end of the evening.

The evening passed quickly and at the end of the rehearsal, he told the children that they had done well. Then he urged them to practice their lines, and reminded them that they only had two weeks to go.

As most of the moms arrived to collect their children, he strode over to Chloe who was putting away everyone's costumes. "How about you come over to the store next time with your mom?" he suggested. "And you can bring your dog with you."

"Mom said he wasn't allowed anywhere near your shop."

He laughed. "I'm sure you'll have him under control next time. But I was telling your mom there are plenty of fields around where I am. I'm sure your dog would like to run there. I can't imagine he gets to stretch those great big legs of his at the moment."

"Can we go there?" Chloe squealed.

"Sure you can."

"Tell my mom."

"I did tell your mom."

"Can you tell her again?"

"I will, but how about you suggest it too?" He didn't understand Chloe's reluctance to speak to her mom.

"She doesn't have time for me."

He bent down so that his face was at her level. "I don't believe that for one moment."

"She doesn't."

"Your mom told me she was excited to take you to Roxy's for some hot chocolate." Chloe rolled her eyes and folded her arms in response. "And she canceled some meetings she had lined up just so that she could spend time with you."

Chloe unfolded her arms.

Unperturbed, he continued. "She's worried that you're getting bored and that you don't like it here. Don't you like it here, Chloe?"

She shrugged. "Chloe?" She looked up at him reluctantly, but before she could answer, a woman he barely recognized came up to him. "I'm here for Chloe Nicholls," she said to him, before turning to the child. "Your mom's running late, so she sent me to get you. Are you ready?"

Chloe looked at him. "Told you she doesn't have any time for me."

Before he could say anything, his cell phone rang, diverting his attention. It was Meredith. "I've run long with a client," she said in a lowered voice. "I can't pick Chloe up and I've sent Joan, Hyacinth's cleaning lady."

"She's just turned up," he answered, as Chloe put on her coat.

"Is Chloe mad at me?" Merry asked.

"She doesn't look too happy."

Merry sighed loudly.

He wanted to set her mind at ease. "I told her she could bring

Spartacus over some time for a run in the fields. That seemed to cheer her up."

"I might just have to hold you to that," said Merry. "Have they left?"

"They're getting ready to go."

"Tell them I'll be another half an hour."

"Okay, hang on."

"That's your mom," he told Chloe. "She's running late."

Chloe's mouth twisted, but she didn't say anything.

"She's busy, Chloe. I'm sure she'll make it up to you."

"She's always busy."

He pressed the phone to his chest so that Meredith wouldn't hear. "She's going to be another half hour."

"That's what she always says."

He didn't know how to respond to that. "I'll see you at the next rehearsal. Good job tonight, Chloe."

He waited until they were gone, and returned to his cell phone ready to talk to Meredith. "They've left," he said, but she had already hung up.

CHAPTER 15

*M*erry rushed home. That meeting with the realtor had gone on too long and she was annoyed with herself. Annoyed that the meeting had taken way longer than she had envisaged and that once again she had put her daughter second.

On top of that, she wasn't too keen on the guy either. He was a smooth-talker, a charmer. Good at spinning stories about the office where he worked where he was one of the youngest partners in the real estate business.

Rourke Halloran. He told her he was a friend of Dylan's, and that he'd seen her at the town hall meeting. She knew he looked familiar from the moment she met him at The Grand Hotel. This reminder might or might not have led to her being extra wary throughout the duration of their meeting.

They had sat in the lobby on the oversized sofas discussing business. Rourke Halloran from Starling Bay Realty was the reason she had been late to pick up Chloe and had needed to call Hyacinth's housekeeper as a last resort.

She rushed home to find Spartacus bounding up to her the moment she stepped inside. "Who's a good boy then, huh? Who's a good boy?" she crooned, stroking the humongous animal as he soaked up her attention.

"You're back." Hyacinth's housekeeper appeared silently out of nowhere and almost frightened her to death.

"Yes," she replied, startled. "I rushed. I didn't want to keep you waiting too long. Where's Chloe?"

"She's in the living room, watching TV."

"Thank you, Joan." Merry slipped her a ten-dollar bill.

"Thank you. I'll be going then. Goodbye."

Merry closed the door after her and leaned against it for a moment. How much she missed her parents. She had never before realized just how much she depended on them to help her out with Chloe. She hadn't envisaged needing anyone's help here, but she hadn't been prepared for the consultations which Hyacinth had lined up for her.

It was unfair to Chloe, and it was beginning to stress her out. It was decided; she would ask her parents to come and spend Christmas with them here in Starling Bay.

Pushing away from the door, she walked into the living room then flopped onto the sofa next to Chloe. "Sorry, honey."

She waited for the usual outburst, or at least some sort of pushback, but Chloe didn't respond. "I don't blame you for being mad at me again. I told you I wouldn't be late and I was worse than last time. I didn't even show up." She let out a sigh. She didn't want this either. "I'm sorry, Chloe. This isn't fair to you, and it wasn't supposed to be like this. I came out here to take it easy."

"Are you going to be sick again?"

Startled, she looked at her daughter's worried face. "No! Of course not. I'm going to be fine."

"Are you?"

"Yes!" She blinked and peered closely at Chloe's face. Her exhaustion back in Boston hadn't been an illness, and she hadn't been sick. She'd only had a few days where she had been unable to get out of bed. She'd been surprised that Chloe had noticed.

But that was in her past.

Even work was in her past.

She had barely thought about Boyd & Meyer.

"I'm not working here, honey," she explained, running her fingers down her daughter's silky hair. "It's more social than proper work, but I do have to meet with these people that Hyacinth sets up meetings for. I owe her for letting us stay here. Maybe I shouldn't have taken up her offer," she mumbled to herself. "Tell me about the pageant," she asked, eager to know.

"Peter's mom didn't look happy."

"Peter's mom?" Merry tried to remember who Peter was.

"His mom helps Dylan out."

That told her right away.

"I remember." Merry nodded. How could she forget Leah? "Why was she angry?"

Chloe shrugged. "Dylan wasn't talking to her much."

"Does he usually talk to her much?" she asked, breezily.

"Peter says Dylan is really nice to him."

"Is he?" She recalled that last time Leah and Peter were waiting with Dylan when she'd been late. If they were waiting, it would be because they were all going home together. Her insides constricted.

"Can we take Spartacus out tomorrow?" Chloe asked. "Dylan said there are lots of fields near his store for him to run around in."

"He's keen on Spartacus running in those fields, isn't he? He suggested that before."

"Can we go?"

"Of course we can. Spart needs a big run." Spartacus lay on the floor, his head lifted in anticipation at the sound of his own name.

"Wanna go for a walk tomorrow?" Chloe asked him. He got up, his tongue hanging out, his eyes gleaming, as if he was about to bound out of the door any second. "Big walk, big boy?" Chloe continued in an excited voice as she crouched on the floor stroking him. He looked towards the door, then back at her, waiting for the signal.

"Don't tease him, Chloe."

"He's bored."

"He thinks we're taking him for a walk *now*."

"Why can't we go now? He's been stuck at home all day."

"It's almost nine o'clock and I'm hungry. We will definitely go tomorrow."

She intended to go through some ads with Dylan, but she couldn't do that if Chloe and Spartacus were in tow. The only way to accommodate everyone and everything was if she hit the fields with Chloe and Spartacus an hour and a half before her meeting with Dylan.

Then she would drop them home, call the babysitter, and return for her meeting with Dylan.

CHAPTER 16

*D*ylan saw Meredith's Jeep pull up, and his heart pitter-pattered. Had they arranged to meet this early?

He didn't think so.

He peered through the blinds of his closed store, wearing his old shirt and clothes and ready to go into his workshop but this was a welcome distraction. The ground was covered in a thin layer of frost, and he wouldn't be surprised if it snowed in the coming days.

But her coming here this early? Had she come to see *him*? Maybe she wanted to talk to him about something? It didn't make sense but it didn't have to make sense. He liked seeing her, and maybe, just *maybe*, she liked seeing him.

In the next moment—while his mind raced towards all sorts of crazy explanations for Meredith's early morning visit—Spartacus bounded out of the Jeep.

Dylan's face fell and disappointment weighed down. So, they were taking the dog for an early morning walk, were they? He felt foolish for daring to think it might have been something else.

He watched the gigantic beast straining at the leash. Chloe

struggled to contain him. Meredith climbed out then and he could have sworn she looked towards the shop.

He shrank back.

There it was again, his heart puttering away. She couldn't see him, because he was behind the blinds and peeking through them, but she had definitely looked, not once, but *twice*, his way.

She took the lead from Chloe and they set off towards the fields. Without thinking, he opened the door and shouted, "Good morning!" They turned around and Chloe waved at him. "Hey, Dylan!"

Meredith nodded at him.

"Taking the dog for a walk?" he shouted, still hovering around the door.

"Come with us!" Chloe shouted back.

He looked towards Meredith, and she nodded. Grabbing his jacket, he locked up and ran towards them.

"Laura will be taking over," he said to Meredith, sensing her disapproval at closing his store.

"I didn't ask."

"But you thought it."

"I'm slowly getting used to the pace of life here."

He chuckled. "Do you mind me coming along?"

"Why would I mind?" Her eyes were shining, and she looked happy. "We don't know the area, and we could do with some guidance from the locals."

Spartacus barked, seemingly annoyed at the interruption.

"Which way?" Chloe asked.

"That way." He pointed straight ahead. "You can't go wrong. Just head straight." They set off with Meredith holding firmly to the lead.

"Can I, Mom?" Chloe held out her hand for it.

"Here," Meredith handed it over to her, and the dog strained even more, making Chloe almost run to keep up.

"You're up early," Meredith commented. She made a shivering noise. She wore a coat and a hat, but out here in the open fields, the cold winds were brutal.

"I can run back and get you a thicker coat," he offered.

"I should be all right. I'll warm up the more we walk."

"Can I let him off the leash, Mom?"

"Are there any roads nearby?" Meredith asked him.

"No. The fields lead to a forest which leads to Lake Ivanhoe."

"That's a pretty sounding name."

He'd never thought of it like that. "It is, I guess, if you like that sort of thing."

"Go ahead," Meredith said to her daughter. The mighty beast raced off at breakneck speed when Chloe took him off the lead. She ran after him.

"He needed this. The poor thing has been cooped up at home the whole time."

He agreed. "This will tire him out."

"Did we disturb you?" she asked.

"No."

"Do you live there, in the store?"

"No. I live about ten minutes in that direction," he said, pointing in the opposite direction to where they were heading.

"You must have started really early today."

"I had some vases to get started on."

"More vases, like the ones on display? They're gorgeous."

"Thanks. I've got an order from a department store out of town. Reed set it up."

"Your friend?"

"You might remember him, he was at the town hall with me that day. Anyway, he's managed to get me a deal to supply twenty of these for the store."

"That's great."

"Yeah, it's pretty good. He looks out for me like that."

"He's a good friend?"

"One of my closest, him and Rourke."

"And he got you this big order?"

"He did. It's hardly big, twenty vases, but it's great. I can't turn it down. Anything helps, right?"

They continued to walk, hearing only the delicate crunch of their feet on the crisp, frost-sprinkled grass. An icy wind bit into his face and hands, and he could imagine Meredith felt it, too. Her cheeks were tinged red.

"You're cold," he stated, seeing the way she'd shoved her hands into her coat pockets.

"I didn't expect it to get so cold out here."

"I did say," he reminded her, "the wind comes in from all sides."

"I'm not used to it. Boston's built up. Even the local parks are surrounded by trees. There's always shelter in places, from the houses and buildings in the surrounding area."

"Do you miss it?"

She stared ahead and was silent for a few moments. "I can't say that I do. Not now. I feel as if I'm finally settling in."

"That's good." The news lifted his mood higher.

She turned and looked at him, and in that moment it didn't matter how cutting the cold air was, her gaze took the edge off it.

"I've noticed something, being here, away from my usual day-to-day life and work."

His hopes rose higher. "What?"

"How much my parents did."

"What do you mean?"

"With Chloe. They help out a lot, they always have."

"Do they live close by?"

"A few blocks away. They moved nearer when…" She looked away, and it was a couple of seconds when she stared straight ahead of her again, offering him a view of her side profile.

"They moved nearer …?" he prompted.

"After my husband died."

"I'm sorry." Of course he knew, but he'd heard it from Hyacinth. This was different coming from Meredith.

She shrugged, acknowledging and dismissing his comment quickly. "They've been the greatest help."

She was finally opening up, finally starting to share with him this tragic part of her life. "How old was Chloe?"

"Seven."

He was trying to figure out how long ago that might have been, trying to get a handle on Chloe's age when she told him. Her daughter and dog were in the distance, but close enough that they could keep an eye on them.

"It happened five years ago."

"I'm sorry." That kind of loss would be life-changing. "Support structures are important," he said, trying to think of something nice to say, a kind word, something soothing, but his mind wasn't cooperating. He couldn't find the right words— words which wouldn't sound trite or meaningless.

Meredith made him feel conscious of himself, as if he needed to impress her and was trying too hard. No woman had made him feel like this before; it wasn't that he was ashamed of himself, but more that he wanted her to see the best of him.

"We're going to start having three rehearsals a week from next week," he said, making the decision suddenly. They had ten days left before the performance, and in previous years he'd only added on an extra rehearsal during the week of the performance. But he only had two weeks left with Meredith, and her threat to leave Starling Bay not long after Christmas had pushed him into this.

"Three?"

Maybe three sounded like too many. It would annoy some of

the parents, "Or two," he said, still mulling it over. "I haven't decided yet, but Christmas is only two weeks away."

"I thought you said it wasn't a Hollywood production?"

"It's not, but an hour a week—and it's less than that by the time the kids settle down—isn't enough." He was telling her a white lie, but it was sort of true. The final performance would still end up with mistakes; children would forget their lines, props and costumes would malfunction, but an extra couple of rehearsals would help.

"Would that cause a problem?" he asked.

"Not at all. Chloe loves being involved in the Christmas pageant, and I'm sure she'd love the idea of having extra rehearsals."

"Are you okay to continue walking?" He nodded in the far distance, but was worried about her getting cold.

"I don't think either of those two will want to head back just yet."

"How about we have our meeting in town?" he suggested. It would change things up from sitting in his kitchen area. He'd left things in a mess because he'd been working until late at night, and he preferred Meredith to not see it.

"In town?" She appeared to think about it. "We could."

"You said you liked Roxy's hot chocolate."

"I do, but Chloe didn't like it much."

"We can go someplace else."

"Or Chloe can order something else. I quite like Roxy's. The only thing is, we won't be able to have a proper discussion, I'm conscious that Chloe might get in the way."

"Chloe's never in the way."

She smiled at that. "You're right, she's not, but at her age she's going to get quickly bored with our discussions. She'll be rolling her eyes and fidgeting."

That wouldn't do. "She could read a book or text her friends," he suggested.

"Oh, she would love that. Are you sure that's okay with you? I didn't want to derail our meeting today seeing that all of our meetings have so far gotten interrupted."

"You didn't derail anything," he assured her.

CHAPTER 17

"*H*ow about the Bombacino?" Merry suggested. "It's warm milk with chocolate sprinkled on top."

"I'm not a baby, Mom."

"I know that."

Her daughter frowned as she looked at the menu at Roxy's.

"What about the hot chocolate? Try it with marshmallows and cream this time?" The last time she'd tried it, it had been without.

"Can I double the marshmallows?"

"Sure you can. You can have anything you want." Merry lingered a moment longer by Chloe's table. Her daughter had elected to sit alone, since 'you and Dylan are talking about work stuff.'

"I can give my own order, Mom. I *am* twelve."

"Of course you can, honey," Merry replied, absentmindedly as she ruffled Chloe's hair.

"So you can go back to your work meeting now."

"Uh, okay." She returned to the table where Dylan sat waiting. After the walk he had grabbed his laptop and they had all jumped into his pick-up, before stopping home to leave Spartacus. Dylan had said he would bring Merry back to his store later so that she could pick up her car. Being carless was a trivial problem compared to the fluttering in her belly. She suddenly wished Chloe was sitting with them.

"I'm having the burger," he announced, as she sat facing him.

"I'm not hungry. I'll just have a hot chocolate."

"Don't you eat at lunchtime?"

"Not much." Lunch had always been a sandwich at her desk when she had been at work. She was a little hungry now but she wasn't going to eat. Not with Dylan sitting across the table from her, looking at her with those big gray-blue eyes.

"Not even a little something?"

"No." This was definitely a sign of something. She'd had the same worry of getting ketchup on her chin, or something stuck between her teeth on those first few dates with Brian. It was impossible to ignore the tingly feeling in her belly, or to completely forget that he had brushed against her—completely innocently, she was sure—as they walked through the door to the diner. Her being self-conscious was further confirmation of this 'pull' towards this man that she was trying hard to understand, and trying hard to pass off as a figment of her imagination.

"At this rate we're not going to get anywhere with your ads," she said, returning to the topic of work.

"It's lunchtime, we have to eat," Dylan insisted. "Don't worry about my ads. I've been plodding along for years before you came along, and I can continue to plod along for a little longer if need be."

"But that's not what you want to do, is it, plod along? I'm here to help."

"You're here to have lunch first, and then we can talk about marketing."

"What would Hyacinth say?"

"Who gives a–" He stopped himself and looked at her. "Who

cares? We went for a walk, my day got derailed in the nicest possible way. Isn't this nice? Or would you rather be elsewhere?"

She could feel herself blushing and looked instinctively at Chloe to see if her daughter had heard. Not that he'd said anything glaringly flirtatious. All these touchy-feely *feels* were probably just in her head anyway. "Let's order, and then I'll walk you through the ad setup and explain the basics. It won't take long, and I can show you on my laptop."

"Okay," he said, in a voice that suggested he would rather not do that. They placed their order—with the aroma of food in the air, she had given in. While they waited, she got out her laptop and talked to Dylan about setting up ads. He was a good listener, and he was smart. He understood, despite him saying that he wasn't a numbers man.

"So, I've set up these few ads here." She showed him the groupings.

"Those are mine?"

"Yes. But I can logon to your account and monitor them. Here's where I've set the daily spend, and this is how you decide how much you want to spend for each click."

He listened, asked a few questions, and seemed to have grasped it all relatively quickly.

"Can we eat now?" he asked, a short while later when the server came over with their food.

"Now we can."

She put her laptop away, pleased that she had managed to spend some time going through the ads with him.

They started to eat.

She watched her daughter do a crossword puzzle which one of the waitresses had given her. She was attempting to do this while also eating her burger. "At least Chloe's not on a device. It's good that the waitress gave her something to do."

"That's Roxy for you. She's always experimenting and trying

out new things."

"She's the owner, I take it?"

He nodded. "The diner's been in her family for years, and she's been taking care of it for a couple of years." He looked around. "She's usually floating around the place, keeping an eye on things, but she must be out today."

Merry had decided that this was her favorite place to be so far. She'd gone to Fellini's last week to meet a client, and she had also been to the Blue Velvet Bar at The Grand Hotel. Neither place had the charm and coziness that Roxy's Diner did. "She's done a great job of it. I love this place. I sneak off here when you're leading the rehearsals."

"I'd rather you stayed there."

She blinked. His comment had surprised her.

"I mean, I would rather you were there...you know... so that you could see how the performance was coming along."

His recovery wasn't so good. "It will be a surprise for me to see it on pageant night," she replied.

"True."

She was curious to see what he had to say. "And, anyway, your friend Leah walks around as if she's the only mom allowed to stay behind."

He raised an eyebrow. "Has she said anything to you?"

"No. She doesn't look too friendly, though."

"You never took her up on the offer to have coffee?"

"I don't get too friendly with people I don't know."

"I must be the lucky exception."

He seemed to be prodding her for answers, too. "But our relationship is based on...on...around business," she pointed out, testing him.

"Is it?" He picked up the menu and flicked through it again even though he had already ordered.

That wasn't a question she wanted to answer. It was a

question to which she wanted the answer, from him. Deflecting, she said, "I wasn't sure if she was...if you were both..."

He made a face. "God, no!"

"Are you taking the day off again?" She heard a man's voice behind her shoulder. By the time she glanced around, he was standing in the middle of her and Dylan.

"Meredith? What are you doing here?"

"Hi," she tried to remember the guy's name. She'd only met him last night. "Rourke," she said, hoping he didn't notice the two-second delay between seeing him and saying his name.

Dylan looked surprised. "You two know each other?"

"We had a meeting last night," Merry answered.

"You met with *him?*" Dylan asked her, then to his friend, "And you never thought to mention it?"

"Since when do I need to report my every move to you?" Rourke shot back. Merry detected undertones of a conflict between the two, and decided not to intervene.

"You don't," Dylan replied calmly, but Merry could tell he was annoyed.

"I was going to tell you when we met," Rourke stated, nonplussed. "It was extremely helpful," he said, turning to her.

"I'm glad you found it useful."

The server appeared at that moment with their food and Rourke moved out of the way. "I'll leave you to enjoy your food. We're meeting later for drinks, right?"

"I've got rehearsals tonight," Dylan replied, looking decidedly unhappy. Was he jealous, Merry wondered? The idea that he might be sent a quiver of excitement through her.

"That's never stopped you before."

"I'll let you know."

"Reed's coming. He won the contract for the old movie theater and he wants to celebrate with a few drinks."

"Maybe not tonight."

"Come on!" Rourke insisted. "What? You're suddenly so busy because you finally have a date?" He grinned widely, but just as the words left Rourke's mouth, he looked sideways at Merry, and then his jaw dropped.

"Oh, I'm sorry." Rourke stepped back, looking shaken. "Sorry…that's not what I meant. I wasn't talking about *you*… I meant…" He turned beet red.

Merry's stomach bottomed out. If he wasn't talking about her, who was he talking about?

"I should go," said Rourke, scratching his chin.

"Yeah. You idiot. You should," Dylan ground out slowly.

Rourke gave Merry an apologetic glance. "Nice to see you again." And then he rushed out as if he couldn't get away fast enough.

What did Rourke mean by Dylan *finally* having a date? And who was he talking about? All sorts of reasons sprang up in her cautious mind, and she didn't want to examine any of them. She felt foolish. Absurd. Deluded. She had allowed herself to think that this man liked her, that he was starting to have some feelings for her. That it might not be only in her head. But she was plainly wrong.

"I should see how Chloe's doing," she said, leaving the table. Her heart was lurching, but for all the wrong reasons. She walked to where Chloe was, desperate to leave. She didn't know this man, not really. No matter how sweet he seemed on the surface, no matter how easy he was to talk to, she had to remember that she barely knew him. For all she knew, he could be a player, a liar, a cheater, or all three.

"Hurry up, sweetie," she said.

"This is really nice, Mom. Want a bite?" Chloe held up her burger, but Merry shook her head.

She had a bitter taste in her mouth, and food had nothing to do with it.

107

The idiot. That was Rourke all along. Lunch had ended abruptly and it was all because of Rourke and his great big galloping mouth. The guy had managed to sour his afternoon in less than five minutes. Dylan had no idea what point his so-called friend had been trying to make, but he could already see the effect it had had on Meredith.

Now she was going to think that he was nothing more than a philanderer. He was no longer wary about the idea that Rourke Halloran, Starling Bay's home-grown Casanova, might have designs on Meredith. She was the type of woman, as far as he could tell, who would run a mile if someone as blatantly flirtatious as Rourke ever approached her.

In all the time Dylan had known him, the guy had never shown any evidence of changing.

Or of growing up.

Meredith had asked if they could postpone their meeting again, and mentioned something about needing to buy some Christmas presents. This had been a sudden development, but he wasn't surprised. He'd seen the look on her face once Rourke had opened his mouth, and he knew the truth. She was already seeing him in a different light.

He offered to drop her back to his store so that she could get her Jeep, but she declined, saying that she and Chloe were going to look around the town square and she would pick it up later tonight.

By then he'd had a call that the clay and paint supplies for his workshop had arrived. He had to drive out to another town to collect them, so it was probably just as well that he didn't have to go all the way to the Clearwater Village.

Driving out of town gave him time to think about this mess. So much for getting marketing expertise in exchange for that time-sucking Christmas pageant. He had another rehearsal tonight, and he was already wary about seeing Merry. He needed to explain Rourke's comment to her, but he knew that there wouldn't be time to do it then.

Those blood-sucking rehearsals. Once this year's performance was over, Hyacinth would be left in no doubt about it being his last show. He had no plans to ever do this again.

Out of him and his friends, he always drew the short straw. They were all trying to make their businesses a success. Reed didn't need much help because the guy was already loaded and successful, and Rourke excelled at his job. Both of his friends were doing well. He was the only one who was struggling.

The artist's path wasn't paved in gold, and he was making things harder on himself by taking on extra commitments that cost him money and did nothing for his bottom line.

He was already choked up with frustration by the time he returned from picking up the supplies and running errands. By the time he headed into the Fitzsimmons Theater, he was already late.

Anger simmered below his calm exterior as he walked into the room full of moms and children. He had missed a large chunk of work today—not that he would have had it any other way—but having to spend his evening leading a rehearsal he didn't want to do, for a performance he had no desire to lead, turned him extra surly.

So when Leah Shriver sashayed across the room to him, he put his hand up and silenced her before she said a word. "I don't have time to listen to anything, Leah. I know we're running late."

"*We're* not late, you are."

He bit down on his molars, reining his temper in. It was only as he took off his jacket, and stood to address the children, that he saw Meredith staring at him. It did nothing to ease his mood.

He grabbed the script, clapped his hands together, and told the children to sit down on the floor. Then he turned to the parents and asked them to leave. To his surprise, Meredith stayed.

This was one of the few times he wished she hadn't. Accepting that the day had gone badly wrong, he steeled himself to get through the next hour. Kids forgetting their lines, props falling apart or going missing, and children whispering and fidgeting were all par for the course.

He just had to get through it.

And he did, but he was always conscious that Meredith was in the audience, watching. He could tell, because he felt her eyes on him. Something had shifted over lunch. Rourke had messed up. Up until then, Dylan had been hoping to gauge what Meredith was thinking, because sometimes, *sometimes*, he got the feeling she was starting to like his company.

The rehearsal worked out fine, and the children were coming along well. They were learning their lines, and by the time Leah had made the costume adjustments, and he'd helped Chloe with the props and lighting, they would have something decent to present on the final night.

"Shall we get your car?" he asked, at the end of the evening when he found Meredith and Chloe waiting for him in the lobby.

They followed him to his truck.

"I'm sorry to put you out like this," said Meredith, climbing in.

"You're not putting me out. I have to go home, don't I?" The store was on the way to his home.

"The angel's costumes came undone," Chloe said from behind.

"Leah's taking them all next week for adjustments. If I forget, will you remember to make sure she takes all the costumes that need fixing?"

"Yup," Chloe replied, then, "Leah's not good at remembering, is she?"

"You noticed, too?" he smiled in his rearview mirror.

"I'll remind her," said Chloe.

He was painfully aware of Meredith's silence. "Did you get all your presents?" he asked her.

"Some of them."

Three words. It was better than a one-word answer.

He tried again, hoping to start an easier conversation. Something work-related. "It's crazy that our meetings keep getting derailed."

"It seems to be the case."

A longer response. It was getting better. "We're jinxed," he commented.

"I'll say."

"Something wrong?" It was obvious, but it wouldn't hurt to ask.

"I should have driven my Jeep back earlier," said Merry.

"Well, you didn't. And it's not a problem," he said quickly, when his words came out harsher than he had intended. Gone was the ease of conversation between them. Now they were being too careful, too stilted, too uneasy.

He turned to her. "I am glad to have company on my way home. It's not a problem, Merry—dith."

111

Chloe giggled behind them.

"What's so funny?" he asked, looking in the rearview mirror again.

"The way you said *Merry—dith.*"

"Why don't you call me Merry?" Meredith asked him.

He wanted to. He would prefer to, because Meredith sounded so formal, and things had been starting to be not so formal between them. "Would you rather I call you *Merry*?"

"Yes. Why didn't you? Only my mother calls me Meredith."

"Because…" he said slowly, knowing that his explanation was going to sound ridiculous. He kept his eyes on the road.

"Because?"

"Because Chloe said you hated Christmas."

"What's that got to do with my name?"

He glanced at her.

"My name has nothing to do with Christmas."

"I wasn't sure, but you hate Christmas, so …"

Silence hung like a spider's web in the air, until Chloe piped up. "Mom hates Christmas because—"

"Chloe." The warning note in Meredith's voice silenced her daughter.

He knew why, but this wasn't the time to bring it up. "You asked," he said, trying to defend Chloe.

Meredith looked away and stared out of the window, and the rest of the journey passed in total silence. He wanted to talk, to explain, to say something, because he didn't like this atmosphere between them, but he didn't know where to start.

Eventually they reached his store and parked. She didn't get out, and neither did he. It was unusually quiet and when he glanced behind, he saw that Chloe had fallen asleep. "Chloe's sleeping."

Meredith turned to look behind. "It's been a long day for her." As she turned back, their gazes locked.

"I'm sorry about this afternoon," he said, broaching the topic now that he had the opportunity.

"Which part of it?"

His brows pushed together, because he hadn't expected that. "Rourke turning up and digging a hole for himself."

"For him or for you?" she asked.

He tilted his head, unclear of what she was referring to. "You've been quiet ever since lunchtime, Meredi—Merry," he said, remembering. "What's on your mind?"

"Your friend, Rourke."

He hadn't been expecting that. He stared directly in front, conscious of the fact that he liked this woman, and he thought she liked him. "You have to be careful with Rourke," he said finally. "He has an eye for pretty women."

"Most men do. I'm not saying that I'm pretty or any—"

"You are," he cut in. "I think you are and … well, I'm just telling you what you need to know."

"I thought he was your friend," she countered, and he wondered why she hadn't said anything about Rourke's comments earlier.

"He is. I know Rourke very well."

"I was going to tell you that I met him last night at a meeting, but I completely forgot."

"I'm not mad at you about that, Merry."

"So you *are* mad about something?" she stated calmly.

"I'm not the only one who's mad, am I?"

She stared at him silently.

"I'm mad at Rourke," he confessed. "I'm mad at him for saying something stupid while we were finally getting to know one another."

"I'm glad you mentioned that. *Why* did he say that?" she demanded, "About you *finally* having a date? Is there some internal joke that I should know about? If you're seeing someone, it's really none of my business…"

"I'm not seeing anyone. Why would you think…" He replayed the conversation in his head. "Did you think he was talking about me and *someone else*?"

"How else was I supposed to take it?"

She had taken Rourke's comment to mean that he was interested in someone else, while *he* had been angry with Rourke for calling out his interest in Meredith. How much damage could a good friend do?

Did he tell her now that he liked her? Maybe not right now. "The guy's been trying to set me up on dates for as long as I can remember," he confessed.

"Oh?"

"He and Reed feel sorry for me."

"Why's that?"

He drew in a breath. "Because I haven't dated anyone for a couple of years now."

"A couple of years?"

He nodded. It didn't feel uncomfortable telling her this. It usually had, in the past, on the one or two disastrous dates Rourke had set him up with. Friends of friends. He'd tried it, and no, thank you. Wasn't for him. As for the online dating stuff, he'd told Rourke what he could do with that. No way was he getting into any of *that* stuff.

He liked this so much better. Getting to know someone slowly, face-to-face. "And there I was thinking you like Rourke."

"Rourke isn't the type of guy I would be interested in."

"No?" he asked, his hopes floating in the air between them.

"No." She lowered her voice. "And I'm not so sure that I should be having this conversation with you now, in the middle of nowhere, with my daughter asleep in the back." She paused, and looked as if she wasn't sure she would continue. Her words had already surprised him because he would never have expected this from her. He wanted to know more but she had always had her guard up and he barely knew much about her. "I don't even know what I'm doing here."

"You're here to pick up your Jeep," he reminded her gently.

Sitting with her in his pickup, having this conversation, he liked that they might have found a way out of the friend zone and were maybe, *possibly,* venturing down a path that could lead to something special.

If things worked out for them.

But it was too soon, and she wasn't here for long. There was so much against them. All he knew was that he had limited time to get his act together and to tell this woman that he liked her.

"I mean," he said, seeing that she was sitting there expectantly, waiting for him to say more. "There's not much to it really, my last girlfriend—"

A soft moan from behind made him pause, and he turned to see Chloe stir.

"Your last girlfriend?" Merry asked, but he was keeping an eye on Chloe.

"She's not going to get a good night's sleep sitting like that," he said, turning to face Merry again.

"No, she's not," Merry agreed. "Chloe. Chloe, get up."

"Don't wake her," he said. It didn't seem fair to wake her up. "I'll carry her to your car."

"Thanks."

He got out, hating that the timing always sucked for them. He had hoped that him opening up to this woman would make her more likely to do the same, so that he could find out more about her.

But this conversation of theirs would have to wait for another time.

CHAPTER 19

*H*e hadn't dated for a couple of years. Merry frowned as she drove, replaying the conversation in her head. That made her feel slightly better.

The question was, *why?*

Because she'd been out of the game for five years now, and she wasn't sure what the rules were, or how to behave, or what to do. She frowned.

"What's wrong?"

"Huh?"

"You're making a face," Chloe told her.

"I am?"

"Did you forget to pick Grandma and Grandpa up?"

"No. That's tomorrow."

Her parents were arriving a week before Christmas and it meant she no longer had to use Hyacinth's housekeeper to babysit Chloe. And it would be nice to have her parents around.

Maybe she and Dylan could go out one evening. For a marketing meeting. She could see how his ads were doing.

A smile spread across her lips. Being around him made her feel all funny. Earlier today it had made her wary, but just now, she felt better for whatever it was he was going to tell her about his past.

At least he wasn't a player.

A player didn't go years without a relationship.

It was like being drunk, but without the alcohol. That was the effect this man had on her.

She analyzed the situation.

Maybe it was the fact that he was new.

Maybe *that* was the attraction. She had been at Boyd & Meyer for years, and had not had the time or energy to think about getting to know anyone again. In the last few years her friends had suggested that she might want to try dating again; her closest friends told her that she couldn't be expected to spend the rest of her life single.

But she hadn't been interested in anyone, and it seemed like too much effort for something she wasn't truly invested in.

And yet, she'd been in Starling Bay for just under a month and she was already having these thoughts about Dylan Fraser.

She liked what she saw in him. She liked that he was thoughtful, and kind, and attentive. Sexy, too. But more than all of these things, it was the way he'd taken to Chloe that had made her notice him first.

How long did she have left in Starling Bay? A couple of weeks? A month at most. Was it worth getting to know him? Or was it better to keep things purely platonic, the way they had been? Soon enough she would return to Boston, and she didn't want to be nursing a broken heart.

She shook her head. This was just a passing phase. She hadn't been around a man for years, and it was perfectly understandable that her senses would turn to mush, and her thoughts became a mess of confusion whenever Dylan was near her. He only had to put on that bomber jacket and her knees would quake.

And yet, she couldn't help but stare at the way his shirts

hugged his biceps, or how much distance there was along his shoulders. He caused her to react in a physical way, and it was something she was not prepared for.

She got home and put Chloe to bed, but she stayed up, feeling restless and thinking about the day, about what Dylan had told her. Even when she finally went to bed, she lay tossing and turning for hours.

As least she wasn't going to see him for the next few days which would be a good break for her. With her parents coming over she blocked out time from meetings and consultations, wanting to spend time with them.

She had managed to explain a few things to Dylan at Roxy's, and talk him through setting up ads and how to tweak them, but she had also warned him to be careful. He promised he would.

Her parents arrived just before lunch, and she and Chloe showed them around the house. They went out for a walk to town, before coming home for lunch and catching up with them.

Maybe because Christmas was around the corner, or because she might have known that her parents had come, but Hyacinth had also stopped calling her. It was just as well because her own boss from work had asked her to follow up on a few things. She was glad for the distraction. There was plenty to keep her mind off Dylan Fraser for a few days.

Until he called her one morning.

"They charged me three hundred dollars for ads yesterday."

She clutched the phone to her ear, not sure if she'd heard correctly. "Three hundred?" That didn't sound right. "Did you change anything?"

"No. I had a look around to check out a few things, but I didn't *do* anything."

He obviously had. She was certain she had set his spend extremely low. "I'll come over and take a look later today. Does that work for you?"

"Later is good."

She made breakfast for her parents, then tried to concentrate on some of the documents her boss had sent her to look over. But she wasn't able to focus as well as she should have, and decided to take her parents out. With Chloe and Spart in tow, they all went for another walk along the bay. Later, they explored the town square where her parents soaked up the atmosphere of the Christmas markets, and bought gifts.

Much later in the afternoon, after she'd dropped everyone at home, she arrived at Dylan's store. She walked into his shop, smoothing down her hair as she smiled at his shop assistant. "Is Dylan around?" she asked casually.

She intended to spend an hour here and had plans to get back home in time to take her parents to dinner. She'd made a reservation at Fellini's. Rourke had suggested it earlier.

"He's in his office," Laura told her.

She knocked at first, but when he didn't reply, she opened the door and walked in to find him behind his desk, wearing a grubby shirt. He looked up, surprised. "Hey," he said, his eyes lighting up as soon as he saw her. "I was wondering when you would come."

After the last time they had met, there was something familiar, and something different about their meeting now. It didn't seem like business, but having whatever *this* was, wrapped under the guise of talking business, she sensed there was so much more going on between them. Words weren't necessary. "I took my parents around the bay."

"How are they?"

"Good." She glanced at him again. "You've been pottering," she commented, forcing herself to look away and scan her eyes around the tiny room.

"Throwing is the word you're looking for."

She raised an eyebrow. "Throwing?"

"You throw clay."

"Throw?"

"Yes. "When you shape clay on the potter's wheel, that's called throwing."

"Sounds like a food fight to me, but with clay. Is that what you do on that spinning thing?"

"Spinning thing, that's cute." He pushed back on his chair and grinned.

"I seem to learn a new thing each time we meet," she declared.

"That goes both ways."

"It's good that we meet, then," she replied brazenly.

"It is good." He looked at her, and she felt her insides heat up. "Sorry about this." He pinched his dirty shirt with his fingers as he rose. "I should have made myself look presentable."

"Presentable?" She cast her eyes over his shirt again. Sure enough, it hugged his biceps, and he'd folded the cuffs up to his elbows so that his forearms were bare. Each time they met, the pull she felt towards him became stronger. No wonder working on the stuff for Boyd & Meyer had paled in comparison to working with Dylan.

Her gaze flickered over him, the sight of his rolled up sleeves, and that dirty shirt, doing more for the rush of blood in her body than a ride on a rollercoaster could ever have. "You always look…presentable…"

He answered with a smile.

"I wanted to come now so that I could get back in time to take my parents out. We're going to dinner tonight at Fellini's."

"Fellini's? They'll like that. It's impressive."

"That's what Rourke said."

"And Rourke would know how to impress people." There was something tight in his tone just then and she didn't understand why. "Come and take a seat," he offered, vacating the chair. "I was taking a quick break to check my ads again. It gets addictive, doesn't it?"

"Wait until you start making money instead of losing it."

He tapped the screen. She sat down and stared at the data in front of her, going over his ads, and the whole time she was conscious of him standing behind her, conscious of the smell of clay, and of his strong, muscled forearms resting lighting on the back of her chair.

It was enough to make her lose concentration.

"Hmmmmm," she murmured, trying to get a handle on the data in front of her. And there it was. "I see what you've done."

"Something *I* did?"

"Yes." She pointed to the budget column on the screen. "You've been playing around with the bids."

"Uh…maybe."

"Not *maybe*, you did."

He bent down so that his head was level with her right shoulder. "Now that you mention it, I was playing around with the daily budget. I was looking at the way that graph changed. I got more eyeballs the more I upped by budget."

"And that's how you ended up spending hundreds of dollars."

He grunted in exasperation.

"You forgot to change it back," she continued. "That's not three hundred dollars overnight, by the way." She wanted to set his mind at ease.

"No?" He sounded hopeful.

"That's three hundred dollars over four days. It's still high for you, because at this stage we're only testing."

"I knew I would hate doing this," he groaned.

She could feel him pressing down on the back of the chair. "I'll set everything back to how I had it," she offered. "And you won't be seeing such crazy ad spend any more."

"Thank you."

He moved away from her, and she was grateful to not have him looking over her shoulder, standing behind her so that she could feel him but not see him.

"I'm not sure this is working for me." He stood in front of the desk with his arms folded. "Maybe we should stop it, before I blow through more money."

She looked up, shaking her head. She'd had a quick look at his metrics and he was doing well given that it was early days. "Don't give up. We've only just started a small ad campaign. We need to test it. Once we get it working, it should deliver results." She wanted to encourage him.

"Then why don't *you* do it for me?"

"Me?"

"I'll pay you a profit of all my sales."

"Sales are going to take some time to translate through. You don't sell anything online so we can't measure who buys what. There's no easy way to tell if the ads are working except if, over time, you see that you're getting more and more people to the store."

"If I wanted to sell online, you'd know how to do that?"

She nodded. She knew the marketing side of it, and she had enough contacts she could set him up with.

"Then help me."

"I live in Boston."

"But you're here now."

"And I'll be returning to Boston soon."

"I'll give you access to my account."

She considered it for a moment. It was doable.

"Who knows," he said, when she didn't answer. "You might like it here and end up staying."

"Never." There was no way she was going to uproot herself and live in Starling Bay. No way.

"Chloe seems to like it here," he maintained.

122

"Chloe likes helping out on the Christmas pageant," she pointed out.

"Just think about it, please?" he begged. "I'll pay you. I'm not expecting any favors."

She didn't know what to say. Being busy and having too much on her plate when she returned to work weren't excuses that came readily, because excuses fell by the wayside. All she could think of was that if she took on what he asked her, it would be an ongoing communication channel between them both.

Her heart was doing its own salsa inside her chest.

"I'm covered in clay," he announced, cutting into her thoughts as he wiped his hand across his shirt. "I should go change."

"What were you making?" she asked.

"Vases. Come and take a look."

"Now? But we were going through this…"

"You fixed the problem with my budget."

"But don't you want me to tell you how to monitor it?"

"It can wait," he replied. He didn't look at the screen, and she could easily see his reluctance to get down into the figures. She wasn't used to dealing with artists. The nature of her work was such that she always had her head in the figures, crunching data and testing lots of different things when it came to advertising and seeing what worked.

It was obvious that Dylan wasn't interested in these things. She could see why he wouldn't be. His passion was in his art, and there was no way she could ever convince him to spend an hour or so each day looking at numbers when he so wasn't a numbers guy.

She followed him through to his workshop, a large open space, not musty and dark as she had imagined, but light and airy. It had worktops all around the edge and a couple of tables on which various mugs and vases rested. And near the center was the potter's wheel.

"You made these today?" She walked over to a table on which lay a line of vases.

He laughed. "No. They're hard, see," he tapped one gently on the table surface. "I made these a few days ago. These are what I made today." He pointed to another, almost identical row of vases on the table next to it.

"These are amazing," she murmured. They looked perfectly proportioned and perfectly shaped. "You're so talented."

"Thank you. Want to see?" he asked, rolling up his sleeves even more.

"You're going to give me a live demonstration?"

He nodded.

"Now?"

"Only for you. Pull up a stool."

She did, and sat nearby, watching him throw a slab of clay onto the middle of the spinning wheel, and then wet his hands and place them into the clay. Then, as if by magic, she watched the clay grow and stretch, spinning around and around in his capable hands, slowly starting to take shape.

"It's all about keeping your hands steady," he told her, looking up at her.

"Concentrate," she cried, worried that he would somehow lose focus if he kept his eyes on her and not the vase.

"Because it might collapse?" he asked, amusement dancing in his eyes.

"Yes." She stared at his hands as he deftly handled the clay.

"Like this?" He deliberately messed it up so that the vase imploded and collapsed.

"No!" she cried in alarm. "Why did you do that?"

He laughed. "You can build it back up again, watch. It's easy." He gathered the clay into a solid lump and moved it to the middle of the wheel again. Then he stopped, and looked at her with a twinkle in his eyes. "You have a try."

"Me?" He had to be joking. There was no way she was going to try that.

"Yes, you." There it was again, his playful smile. Had it always been playful, because she'd never noticed it quite like that before?

"No, I can't." For a start, she didn't want to get her hands dirty, and, most importantly, she wasn't a creative person. She didn't have a creative bone in her body.

"Yes, you can," he replied, dismissing her objections easily. She blinked and stared back at him. Had his eyes always been this blue? She could have sworn they were gray the other day. Where was Spartacus when she needed a beast to come crashing through the door and upset the state of play?

"No. Trust me. I can't. I really can't. I'm more comfortable with calculators and spreadsheets…really."

He didn't seem to be paying any heed to her objections, as he wiped his hands on a cloth, and then moved his stool out of the way and stood opposite her.

"I'll help you. Come on. Here," he walked away to one of his cupboards, pulled something out and walked back to her. "Put this on, it will stop your clothes from getting dirty."

He clearly wasn't listening, and he had every intention of making her do this. She sensed that he wasn't going to stop until she complied. Huffing to signify her disapproval, she grabbed the apron and slipped it over her head. "It's going to be lousy."

"It doesn't matter if it falls down in a heap. I can fix it."

She sat down on the stool, an image of Patrick Swayze and *that* scene from *Ghost* suddenly flew into her mind, making her fidgety. It was the last thing she needed to remember, standing here with a hunk of her own. Dylan shook his head. "No sitting."

"We're standing?" she asked.

"It's easier to stand." He turned on the pottery wheel and dribbled some water over the clay, and then with his fingers and

125

with the wheel slowly spinning, he manipulated the slab until it started to grow again. "You just gently apply pressure, a little here and there, and gently make the clay thinner, like this…"

A peculiar sensation came over her; a tightening of her chest, and a feeling of giddiness. It was nothing like the panic she'd experienced at work. This was something else. Warm, and fluttery, and it fanned from her belly outwards. Thank goodness he was standing opposite her, and not right behind like. Not like Patrick had.

"Now you try."

"What?" The warm, fluttery feeling vanished, leaving her hot, and bothered, and excited. "What do I do?"

"What I just showed you."

"I wasn't paying attention." Long-buried feelings rose inside her, just like the vase had risen from the slab of clay.

"Let me guide you," he murmured, his voice soft and sexy.

He could guide her all he wanted if he spoke to her with that voice.

Meredith Nicholls, pull yourself together!

"Like this," he said, blanketing her hands gently with his. Her heart rate rocketed. Completely oblivious, he moved her fingers gently. "Light pressure," he said, dropping his voice to a whisper.

She let out a breath, relieved that he was standing across from her, and that a pottery wheel separated them. The feel of his hands on hers was electric, even though their hands were covered with wet clay. She wondered what it might feel like to have those hands on her …

She blinked, and swallowed, and tried hard to concentrate, to look at the clay taking form but her body seemed to have a mind of its own.

"See." The vase elongated easily and beautifully in his hands. He moved them away, so that only her hands remained. "There you go, *you're* doing it now."

126

"It's going to fall," she said, unconvinced. Her mind wasn't on the clay. It was on *him*.

"You okay?" he asked. She heard the concern in his voice. "Don't worry, you're not going to break it."

"It's going to fall," she cried.

"It's not. Trust me."

"It is!"

"Then let it. What's the worst that could happen?"

She kept her hands around the clay, and it didn't implode. He was right. The clay grew and stretched, and the vase became taller, rising out of her hands. "It's working!" she cried, then looked up at him.

"See? It's not so difficult, is it?"

But then it started to wobble, and she panicked. "Dylan," she said, not taking her eyes off the clay. "Help!"

"What's the worst that could happen?" He was by her side now. "I'm going to slow it down. Steady." The wheel ground to a stop, and she looked at the almost perfect vase in awe. "I made that," she gasped. "I don't have an artistic bone in my body."

"Here's proof that you do."

He was right. "I never thought I could." She was surprised by what she had just made.

"You never know until you try."

Their hands were still on the wheel, and for a split second, she looked up at him, and their fingers touched. Sparks ignited all over her body. He dipped his head and stared at her with those bluer-than-bluer eyes. Her gaze fell to his lips, so inviting, so tempting, and a fire kindled in her belly. When he slid his fingers over hers, the feel of the wetness was so seductive and intimate, that she let out a tiny breath.

She lifted her face and they stared at one another. His gaze dropped to her lips, and her eyes followed suit as she stared at his mouth. A yearning intensified inside her. It had been so long since

127

she had felt this level of excitement. An urge spiraled out from deep inside her, and she was overcome by the desire to feel his lips on hers, and his arms around her.

"Would it be wrong of me to kiss you?" His voice was low, seductive.

Her heart missed a beat. "No," she murmured, breathless.

"Because I've been wanting to kiss you—"

"Then kiss me," she whispered, her voice hoarse. His good old-fashioned chivalry was trying her patience.

And then he did. Their lips had barely brushed together when footsteps made them spring apart.

"Sorry to interrupt, but there's an urgent call from someone at the department store. It's regarding the vases." If Laura had any idea what had taken place, she seemed unfazed. "The man was quite insistent," she said apologetically.

Dylan moved away, wiping his hands on a cloth. "I'll take it in my office. There's a sink in the corner," he said to Merry, before disappearing.

She stood alone at the potter's wheel, knowing she would never look at this item in the same way again. Then, she tried to stay still for a few seconds, composing herself, trying to get over the thrill of what had just happened.

Patrick Swayze had nothing on Dylan Fraser.

CHAPTER 20

*H*e had *almost* kissed Meredith yesterday.

What they'd had wasn't even a proper kiss, more like a light peck on the lips, but it *had* happened. It hadn't been his imagination.

And he wished he could have kissed her *properly.*

He'd had to leave soon after the call from the home furnishings store. They wanted a delivery of vases before the forecasted snow set in during the weekend. He hadn't wanted to leave—what he wanted was to take the rest of the day off and spend it with Merry—but he'd had no choice.

He returned back to his workshop after taking the call, wanting to rekindle the magic he and Merry had just created, but she seemed eager to leave.

He understood. This had been unexpected, and he didn't want to push things. Merry's flushed face and gentle smile told him she needed time to process what had happened between them. And so she left.

But the rest of the day had been slow. He had been busy going about his daily errands, but his mind had been preoccupied with thoughts about Merry.

Happy thoughts, nonetheless.

It had been years since he'd had any such thoughts about a woman.

When rehearsal night came around again, he found himself eagerly looking forward to it for a change. The room was full of mothers dropping their children off, and he looked around, hoping to catch sight of Meredith. Instead, he saw Leah, and she gave him the evil eye from across the room. Ignoring her completely, he turned to see Meredith come towards him wearing the same kind of smile that he probably had on his face.

"Hey," he said, resisting the urge to take her hand. It had only been the lightest brushing of their lips yesterday but it had started off a chain reaction inside him the likes of which he hadn't been prepared for. Not only did he want to take her hand, he wanted to put his arms around her and hug her close.

"Hi." Her perfect smile just made things better. Made it harder for him to resist, and when she was so close that there was only a shoulder's width between them, he took her hand tenderly. She looked surprised, but she didn't wrench it away.

"I wish you would stay here during the rehearsal."

She angled her head. "What role would you have given me?"

"Something backstage, costumes or props."

She gave him a smile that made him forget where he was for a moment. "Why?"

"So I could have you here the whole time, instead of just at pick-up and drop-off times."

She leaned in and whispered into his ear. "We can meet outside of rehearsal time, you know." Then she pulled away, her eyes flashing and twinkling, and making him wonder where she had been all his life.

"That's true. I could always give you another pottery lesson."

"I'm a good student."

"The best," he replied, wishing he could have that time with her all over again, have her working with him in the workshop.

A silence fell as they looked at one another. "I recall we were in the middle of something," he said, squeezing her hand.

She squeezed it back. "A marketing meeting, I believe."

"My son doesn't like his costume." Leah's voice screeched into his ear. She wasn't shouting, but she had that banshee-esque voice and right now it grated on his nerves like inch-long nails scraping along a blackboard. He turned to her. "He's a donkey, Leah," he said, feeling sure they'd had this conversation before.

"But he's complaining that it is hot. He can't breathe."

"He's no different than the sheep."

"He can't wear anything over his head."

"Then I'll get him to hold up the star."

She glared at him.

"What's your daughter doing?" she asked, turning on Merry like a viper.

"She's helping backstage."

He didn't like Leah pulling Merry into the disagreement. "What Chloe does has nothing to do with you, Leah."

"You shouldn't have favorites," she hissed, before turning on her heel and leaving.

"She doesn't like me," said Merry.

"She doesn't like that I'm showering you with attention."

"Is that what this is?"

"Me showering you with attention?" he asked, suddenly aware that in a room full of noisy people, it felt as if it were just the two of them. He wished he didn't have to do this tonight. He wished he could whisk her away somewhere, not so that they could get up to anything, because that wasn't how he operated, but because he wanted to spend time with her and get to know her better. All they had were meetings, and his time with her was never enough.

"Are they your parents?" he asked, seeing Chloe with an older couple.

"That's them. I'll introduce you at the end, if you want."

"Sure."

"I should go. I've got another business meeting at the hotel now."

"Rourke?" His gut twisted at the thought.

She placed a hand on his forearm. "No, Reed Knight."

"He's a friend of mine," he said, somewhat relieved. "You might have seen him that night at the town hall meeting."

"I don't remember much from that night, aside from you laughing at me when I got up on stage."

He rubbed his thumb over her hand. "I wasn't laughing at you. I was shocked to see that the owner of the beast was Starling Bay's new marketing manager."

"Oh, please, no. Don't call me that." She rolled her eyes, exaggerating her disdain. "What's he like, this Reed Knight?"

"He'll pick your brains for ideas, but he doesn't need too much help. The guy is a smart businessman."

"Apparently, he has plans to renovate the old movie theater. I didn't even realize that the old building next to Fellini's was a movie theater. The architecture is beautiful."

"It closed down years ago because people weren't visiting, and the upkeep cost too much. Reed has this idea of fixing it up and making it a landmark building here. It would do wonders for Starling Bay."

"That sounds amazing," she said.

"It's a shame you won't be around to see it when it's ready."

She gave him a wistful look.

"Unless you come back here, occasionally," he suggested.

"I'm going to try to make it back in time to pick Chloe up," she replied, leaving his suggestion hanging in the air, unanswered. "But if I'm late my parents will be here."

His heart sank. He'd been hoping to catch her again at the end. Time was moving on and he needed to start the rehearsal. "I have to go," he told her, and she slowly let go of his hand, except that he grabbed one of her fingers lightly. "Meet me," he pleaded. "Meet me tomorrow."

"Tomorrow?"

"If you're not busy."

"I'm not sure…"

"You were going to show me something to do with the bids. You don't want me to blow through hundreds of dollars again, do you?" he asked, sensing her hesitancy. If he made it about the business, she would come running. "There are some things I'm unclear about." It was partly a lie, there were *many* things about the ads he wasn't clear about, but that wasn't why he wanted to see her tomorrow.

"Okay. I'll come over."

It was settled.

The next day, he woke up with a smile; something he hadn't done in a while. When Meredith's Jeep pulled up in the parking lot, he strode out to greet her. The fresh snow, soft and velvety, crunched beneath his footsteps. The sun was out and the snow glittered all around.

She got out of the car, smiling. "Is this part of the service, you coming out here to greet me?"

"Only for special customers."

"I'm honored. You're making me feel special."

"You are special. I just didn't know it before."

She smiled. "You're quite the charmer."

He couldn't help but smile back. In fact, the sight of her always made him smile. "Rourke's the charmer. I'm the artistic dreamer, but I wear many hats."

"I'm beginning to see."

133

He moved over to the hood, wanting to take a closer look. "Could I take a look?"

"Where?"

"Under the hood."

"For what?"

"For whatever it is that's making your Jeep stall."

"Aw," she waved her hand. "Don't worry about that. It doesn't happen much."

"I don't mind checking it out." The fact that it had happened once was one time too many. But he was aware that he might be overstepping his boundary, and he didn't want to push it.

"I was hoping we could go for a walk in the snow. I like it when it's freshly fallen. As you see, I came prepared." She pointed to her boots. He looked her up and down; she looked a pretty picture, with her dark blue coat and matching woolen hat with a brown furry bobble at the top. She fit right into the scenery, and a walk in the woods with her right now? He would be stupid to turn that down.

"Let me get my jacket."

"Great." She seemed excited and something in her tone made him wonder if he'd missed something.

She felt giddy. Foolishly giddy. Like a schoolgirl. Ever since that day in his workshop, revisiting that kiss made her breathing go funny. She'd barely been able to sleep. Maybe that was a slight exaggeration. It probably had more to do with not having been near a man for years, than it was to do with Dylan's magnetism, but this feeling in her stomach, these random cartwheel motions that had been swirling around inside her on the drive here, weren't her imagination going into overdrive.

She and Dylan *had* touched lips. Even driving out here to see him, her heart had started to pound, *the entire way.* She couldn't stop thinking about him, and grinning like a crazy fool.

And now that she was here, she'd concocted the idea of going for a walk because there was no way she'd be able to concentrate; not sitting so close to him in that small office of his. Even if she asked to hold the meeting in his kitchen area it wouldn't do. There was no safe zone around Dylan Fraser.

She was in trouble.

Going for a walk might help to calm her down, might help to get her into the zone; the serious, working zone. Instead of wondering what it might be like to have him kiss her, properly this time.

She couldn't suppress the smile when he came out dressed in that too-sexy bomber jacket, wearing that all-too-sexy grin.

"Ready?" she asked, even though any idiot with half a brain could see that he was.

"I like this idea of yours."

"Oh?"

"It's always good to get some fresh air in. It's too easy for me to get holed up in my workshop and not see daylight."

"You're the living embodiment of the artistic recluse."

"Am I?" he asked, looking unconvinced.

She swallowed. That had been a downright lie. There was nothing artistic or reclusive looking about this man. Of course, when his sleeves were rolled up, and he wore an old shirt caked with clay and paints, and she caught a glimpse of those forearms...that was a different matter. "Have you always lived here?" she asked, thankful that an easy question had just come to her.

"I was born here, but I moved to LA in my twenties. The acting bug bit me."

"Acting?" Oh yes. Yes, yes, yes. She could see him in that profession.

135

"But it was hard to break into it, and I ended up waiting on a lot of tables and doing lots of odd jobs. It was a soul-sucking experience, if I'm honest with myself."

She looked at him, a twist of sadness tightening inside her. "Is it really that hard?" *Even for someone who looks like you?*

"It's brutal. I managed to get some work doing voice-overs in commercials for a while but that eventually dried up. I knew it was time to find another way to earn a living, so I took a few courses and went back to making things. I'd always loved doing that but as a side hobby. In the end, I moved back here, about four years ago, and started the store."

"You've done well, considering." Many new companies failed in their first five years.

"I want to do better."

"I can help you do better." She was motivated to get things rolling for him.

"Tell me about you," he said, rubbing his gloved hands together.

"Me?" She hated talking about herself. "It's cold, isn't it?" she commented, even though she had wrapped up, she could feel the chill biting through.

"Want to go back?"

She had calmed down now. Her man-famine seemed to affect her the most when she was away from him, but this, talking to Dylan now, and being with him, seemed almost natural. It surprised her how easy this was. She shook her head. "It's nice being out. I'd rather stay out here for a while."

"We can head into the forest, if you want. You won't feel the wind there so much. So, tell me about you," he said, not missing a beat.

She did. As they continued to walk she told him about how she had worked up the ranks at Boyd & Meyer, and how hectic her work was, and he listened, and paid attention, asking her questions along the way.

It was soothing, and easy, opening up to him, telling him about her life and hearing about his. Catching glimpses of one another's lives put things into context, and the more she discovered about him, the more she found herself looking at him in a different way.

They headed into the forest and there was no sound to be heard except the crunching of the snow beneath their feet, and the occasional rustle of bushes as Dylan pushed the wayward leaves away. At points where the pathway was narrow and only for one person, he would go in front and she would follow—and admire the view of him from behind, her heart still pitter-pattering beneath her layers, and beneath her chest. Most of the time, there was a well- defined path and the two of them could walk together.

After they had swapped stories about their jobs, and ambitions, the conversation fell silent. She wondered what he was thinking. There was still that thing, hanging over them from the last time. The *almost-kiss*, and their conversation from before that day. Each time they seemed to get closer, something always pulled them apart.

"You were saying that you started the store four years ago?" she asked, hoping to somehow steer him back towards that conversation the other night where he had been about to say something about his last girlfriend.

"Uh, yeah. Four years ago."

Just then they came out of the woods and before them lay the lake. It hadn't yet iced over, and the blue-green water shimmered under the sun. "Oh," she gasped. "That is stunning."

"It's a beautiful sight, isn't it?"

They faced the lake in silence.

"You should see it in the summer," Dylan said.

She didn't say anything. She wouldn't be here in the summer.

"You can always come back in the summer," he suggested, as if he had read her mind. "Lots of people do. Starling Bay is a great place for a vacation."

"I'll have to think about it."

"I hope you do."

Was he just saying that because it was the normal thing to say, or was he saying that because he meant it? "I'd...I'd like that."

"So there's a chance I might get to see you again?"

Now her heart tripped another beat. "Maybe."

He turned to face her, that dimple in his chin more beguiling than ever. "I would like to see you again, Merry. That is, if you'd like to see me again."

He'd said it out aloud. This wasn't business talk. It was heart talk. A declaration of wants and desires, and it made her insides jump for joy. "I would."

"You would what?" He took off his glove and stroked her face.

"I would...I would like to see you again."

"I was hoping you'd say that."

She stared at him, at his dimple, his eyes, and his full lips. Her pulse, and heart, began to strike up a rhythm, matching the one in her ears, of the blood pounding. She was going to have a seizure if he kept on stroking her cheek like that. His finger soft and warm, was doing things to her that she didn't know a digit was capable of doing. And when he brushed his thumb over her lower lip, it electrified every single cell south of her belly. "I believe we were interrupted the other day."

She held her breath. If she had any doubt as to whether he'd been thinking about that moment, the look in his eyes told her all she needed to know.

"Laura," she said, attempting humor, and rolling her eyes.

He blinked, as if she'd suddenly lost him by mentioning his assistant. "Would it be okay if I kissed you ag—"

"Yes please do." She said, the words rushing out of her mouth. Before she could blink his lips were over hers. Soft, and gentle, just lips, at first, and then his arms wrapped around her, and he pulled her close. She moaned in appreciation. Just the idea of being wrapped up in his arms, with his lips and body pressed close were enough to make her dizzy. And then he pulled away.

"Yes please do?" he asked, tilting his head, his voice teasing.

But before she could say something back, his lips were on hers again, and this time she settled in closer, as if she was sliding into a comfy, big sofa and settling in for the night. Slowly, ever-so-slowly, his tongue slipped between her lips, gentle, and exploring at first. She savored the sweet, silky taste of him as he deepened the kiss. She moaned into his mouth, her nerve-endings in flames as their tongues met, and their bodies pressed tighter. It was soft and floaty, like being on the surface of a gentle wave, and then it sped up, turning feverish, and they took greedily. This was brand new all over again, the newness of being with a man who excited her, and getting to know his scent, and feel and touch. She clung to him because she didn't want to let go.

But they pulled apart, because they needed to breathe. She hadn't been kissed like that for years. Many, many, many years. Their gazes locked and held for a forever moment, and they breathed hard, holding hands now. She waited for her heart to stabilize, waited for the dizzying feeling in her body to subside.

"That's a kiss I'll never forget," she gasped, breathless. Smiling, he squeezed her hand. "It's a kiss *I'll* never forget."

"Maybe we should get back?" she suggested, worried that she could get used to doing nothing but this for the next few hours.

Wordlessly, he tugged at her hand, and they walked back through the forest, but every once in a while, they would stop and kiss, as if it was the first time they had ever.

CHAPTER 21

"She definitely knows her stuff," said Rourke.

His friend had somehow managed to steer the conversation over to a discussion about the 'marketing expert.' Not that Dylan minded. He was missing out on seeing Merry tonight, so talking about her seemed to be the next best thing, even if it was with these two. He wasn't ready to tell Reed and Rourke anything yet. It was still early days, and after yesterday, after finally getting to kiss Merry properly, he hadn't been able to think about anything else but her.

"She's good," Reed commented. "Did you know she works for Boyd & Meyer?"

"Who?" Rourke asked.

"It's a department store in Boston," Dylan replied.

"She gave me her business card," Reed continued. "I'll hold onto it."

"What do you need it for?" Dylan asked, curious, not that he was worried about anything now.

"It never hurts to know a marketing expert."

"I've got her business card, too," Rourke chimed in.

"I'm dubious about *your* reasons for wanting it." Dylan

examined his friend's expression closely. "She's a single mom. That's way too much for you to take on, I think."

Rourke shrugged. "She's got a pretty face. But don't worry, I won't get in *your* way."

"Oh?" Reed glanced at both of them before his gaze settled on Dylan. "Do you have something to tell us?"

"No," he replied, trying to sound casual.

"I didn't know she was a single mom," said Rourke.

"You find out all sorts of information at the pageant rehearsals," Dylan replied, hoping this explanation would suffice.

"How's that going?" Reed asked.

"We're almost at the end." Ordinarily, he would have been pleased about it but the rehearsals had been a way of seeing Merry, and now he would have to find other ways. 'Dating' was an alien word to him. He didn't like the idea of labeling what they had, or what they might be. Yet, being with Merry was easy; holding hands and talking came naturally. Thinking about it, their whole getting-to-know-one-another had been effortless. And now once the pageant was over, he would have to find other ways of getting to see her. The clock was ticking and he knew she would soon leave Starling Bay.

"No more Leah Shriver then?" Rourke teased.

"There never was *any* Leah Shriver," he shot back.

"She's only there because of you, you know that, right?"

"I'm not interested. Why don't you put her out of her misery and *you* ask her out?" Dylan suggested.

"I'd rather take a dive in a sewer."

"Nasty," muttered Reed.

"I hope you're both coming to the show," said Dylan.

"I'll be there. I can't vouch for Olivia, though."

"That fiancée of yours is always jet-setting off to one place or another. Where is she going now? To another party?" Rourke asked.

"Damned if I know," Reed growled.

"How's business?" Dylan asked, noticing that something was up.

"It's good. Business is good. I can't complain. I'm looking forward to the movie theater renovation."

"Meredith was impressed that you were taking that on."

"Was she?" asked Rourke, his eyebrow lifting slowly. "Was she impressed by you, by any chance?"

Dylan shook his head. Sometimes, talking to Rourke was like dealing with a teenager.

"Are there any comedic elements to this year's performance?" Reed asked. Something or other was always going wrong at the pageant. It was a given.

"The kids have half remembered their lines. The costumes are almost there, and we've got the same props," said Dylan. "If there are any comedic elements, you'll see them on the night. The children often like to surprise me."

"At least their parents will enjoy it," said Reed. "We'll be there for moral support."

"Give it time. Your and Olivia's firstborn will get the main role as soon as he's able to talk. Isn't that right?" Rourke elbowed him in the rib, winking, then, "Isn't that her?" he asked, suddenly staring at the lobby. They all turned to look and that was when he saw her. Merry had walked out of the restaurant and was in the lobby.

"Hey!" Rourke got up and raised his hand, waving at her.

"What are you doing?" Dylan hissed. He didn't think Merry would want to come over and talk to them.

"Meredith!" Rourke shouted.

She turned, and looked puzzled at first when she saw Rourke, but then her gaze slipped to Dylan, and her smile widened. They locked gazes for an instant, until she looked at his friends, and walked towards them.

"Hi," she said, her gaze lingering over Dylan for a few seconds.

"Hey," Dylan replied, wishing it could be only the two of them. "I didn't know you were going to be here tonight."

"My mom and dad wanted to eat out. They've already been to Fellini's so I thought we'd try the restaurant here."

"I've given your details to my friend from Vermont," Reed told her. "You might hear from him in the next few days."

"She's got a regular full-time job to go back to," Dylan replied. "This general advice was only meant to be for a few people." He felt suddenly protective about her and didn't like the way people—including his friends—seemed to be piling her with more and more work. She had come here to take a break from it all.

"I was only trying to help," Reed said.

"It's fine," Merry replied, throwing Dylan a cautionary glance.

"Dylan says you've helped him with his advertising," Rourke cut in. "He says you showed him how to use social media. Well done, I didn't think it would be possible to get this guy to use those platforms."

"He's a good student," Merry said.

"She's a good teacher." He could feel his friends exchange a knowing stare, and he was just short of kicking them under the table.

"He seems to have come a long way," exclaimed Rourke. "There was a time when he couldn't even get his dating profiles set up properly."

"His what?"

Dylan glared at him.

"What I meant is…" said Rourke, trying desperately to climb out of the huge hole he'd just dug for himself. "He's just not … he's not …he's not so great pushing himself."

Merry looked at him and he could see the light fade from her eyes.

"What he means to say," said Reed, glaring at Rourke on his behalf, "is that Dylan's a nice guy. We can vouch for him."

"They…they're just being silly," Dylan said, trying to make things better before he lost her.

"My parents are waiting for me," she said, indicating the restaurant behind her. "I'd better go."

He almost got up, not wanting her to leave and knowing that some damage might have been done, no thanks to his friend's stupidity.

"I'll see you around," she said, then slipped away quickly, but she went off in the direction of the washrooms.

"Thanks," he said, snapping at his friends. "Dating profile?" he barked at Rourke. "What the hell were you thinking? I didn't go through with that."

"That was the point I was trying to make!"

"Thanks for ruining things."

"Ruining things?" asked Reed quietly. His forehead puckered. "You like her, don't you? It's happened, Dylan Fraser has finally found a species of the female variety that lives up to his idealistic standards."

"Can you stop it?" he growled.

"Does she know?" Reed asked.

"Does she know what?"

"Does she know that you like her? Because we know how slow you can be. If it was up to Rourke, he'd have been on the tenth date by now."

"That's because he," Dylan nodded at his friend, "is Starling Bay's resident Lothario. I don't want to take that title away from him."

"You're missing out," said Rourke, his lips stretching into the widest of grins. Dylan shifted uneasily in his chair. It made him want to punch Rourke. He wasn't ordinarily a hotheaded type of guy. He didn't lose his temper, didn't blow up over trivial matters, but it had taken weeks for him to acknowledge and then do something about his feelings for Meredith Nicholls.

That kiss.

That kiss was a sign that things were heating up between them.

He wasn't sure how much it would take to fix that damage, or how he would get to have her to himself so that he could assess it.

Nothing major had happened, but he knew Merry. He had come to know of her past now, and he knew it wouldn't take anything major to push her away again. Something as simple as one of Rourke's stupid comments was enough to ruin things for him.

"Hey, where are you going?" he heard the guys shout out after him, but he was up and out of his seat as soon he saw Merry returning from the washroom. Her face was set, hard and unyielding, just like that first time Spartacus had steamrolled into his store.

"Hey," he said, reaching for her arm. She turned around at his touch, then moved her arm away. "Sorry about that," he said.

"About what?"

"About Rourke and what he said."

"About your dating profile?" She forced a laugh, then shrugged. "What about it?"

"I don't... I didn't go ahead with it."

"It's ...nothing. I don't know why you're making such a big deal of it."

"Because I can see you look upset."

"I'm not," she insisted. "I have to go. My mom and dad are waiting for me."

"I'll see you tomorrow?" he asked, but she had already slipped away from him.

With a sinking heart he returned to the table. Reed, pensive, and quiet, stared back at him as if he was waiting for him to say something. Rourke, transparent and ignorant, sat there smirking. "Did I see right?" he asked. "Did you...did you just go and make a move on that woman?"

"I think the move was already made," replied Reed, "Until you opened your big mouth and landed him in it."

"Me?" Rourke retorted. "What the hell did I do?"

Enough, thought Dylan. He'd done enough.

CHAPTER 22

"Who was that man you were talking to?" her mother asked casually.

"Which man?" Merry knew perfectly well who her mom meant; her mother had eyes like a hawk. What surprised her was that her mother had waited until they had returned home before saying anything.

"The one in the hotel lobby."

Merry turned up the TV volume slightly, and shushed her mom, pretending to have developed a sudden interest in the food chopper infomercial that had come on.

"Meredith?"

"What, Mom?" she cried, slightly irritated. It had been bad enough her mother asking if Chad Bostwick had kissed her back when she was fourteen, but to have a similar-ish conversation at this age didn't feel right at all.

"Don't 'what, Mom' me, Meredith. You know perfectly well who I mean. The nice-looking gentleman. They all looked rather nice, but the one you were talking to, he looked especially handsome."

Trust her mother to say something like that. Merry ground

147

down on her teeth, forced into a conversation she didn't want to have. "Oh, him," she replied, acting dismissive. "He owns a pottery gift store." She kept her attention on the TV.

"And does he have a name?"

"Dylan. Dylan Fraser."

"And is he single?"

"Mom! How should I know?" She wished her mom would go to bed, or leave her in peace. It had been a mistake to sit down and watch TV with her. But her mind was still running through the conversation with Dylan and his friends earlier. He always seemed slightly different when he was around his friends. It had been the same that first time she had seen Dylan with them at the town hall.

The Dylan she knew on a one-on-one basis was not the same man when he was with his friends.

Or maybe she was being paranoid about it, and him, and questioning everything now that they had moved forward?

She wasn't used to this new situation she now found herself in. Suddenly, being out of her comfort zone felt dangerous. Maybe her seeing Dylan differently was her way of pushing him away?

"You're a clever girl, Meredith, I'm sure you could elicit the information out of him one way or another. He wasn't wearing a ring."

"Where were you watching from?" She had a vision of her mom looking at her through a pair of binoculars.

"I was still sitting at the table, Meredith. No need for you to look so shocked. I had a perfectly good view of you both."

"He's a friend. An acquaintance. Hyacinth insisted I give him a consultation."

"He was stroking your arm."

"Mom!"

"Meredith, I'm your mother. Talk to me."

148

No. No. No. No.

Merry flicked through the TV channels absentmindedly, needing to do something with the irritation that was building up inside her. "Mom, please. Just drop it. There's nothing going on." For the first time, telling a white lie to her mom felt liberating. And necessary.

"It seems to have done you the world of good."

"He's just a friend!"

"Being here, I meant. Aside from right now, you've seemed a lot calmer, Meredith. More relaxed, and laidback. Your father and I noticed it as soon as we arrived."

Merry was thankful to move on to a different subject.

"It's been different."

"I can see that. You look a lot better. You seem calmer, and I'm not surprised. Boyd & Meyer work you to the bone."

"They don't do anything to me, Mom. I choose to do those long hours." Although, Dan Shepworth had called her yesterday, asking if she might be able to return to Boston for a day or two this week. There was the usual end-of-year meeting with the board members, and Dan told her that he needed her there, if possible. Reading between the lines, Merry gathered that her replacement, a temp named Kate, had messed up a few things at work, and these issues needed addressing. Her boss had also reminded her about the usual pre-Christmas cocktail party at his house.

"Have you ever stopped to think what you're running away from?"

"I need to work, Mom. Brian's not here and someone—"

"I know, honey. I know." Her mother's voice turned soft. "You're still young, and you're not broke, you never have been. You didn't do those long hours out of necessity to put food on the table. I know it was your way of coping, Meredith, but it's been five years now. I would hate for you to do nothing but work, and miss out on the important things in life."

Merry clamped down on her teeth, the muscles along her jaw tightening. She didn't need her mom to spell out what these things were. It wasn't only her relationship with Chloe she had to fix, but she had to wonder about the type of future there was for her.

Until Dylan Fraser, she hadn't had to think about it.

Meeting him had started a ripple effect.

Even the thought of returning to Boston for a few days hadn't appealed as much as it would have done in the past.

At least it hadn't, until this evening. But now, in light of what she'd heard earlier today, perhaps a little distance between her and Dylan would not be such a bad thing.

"I might have to go to Boston for a few days," she announced.

Her mother's eyes widened in disbelief.

"But we've only just arrived here. We've come to spend Christmas with you here."

"And you still will. It would only be for a few days."

"What on earth for?"

"The person standing in for me seems to have made a mess of some things. I need to go back and fix things."

"Can't they do without you?"

"Apparently not." It was a good position to be in. Indispensable. But it no longer seemed as important.

Her mother's face twisted. "You were supposed to be taking a break from work," she protested. "I wish they would let you rest."

"Hyacinth's keeping me busy."

Her mother looked cross. "I told her you needed a break."

"She's been good," said Merry quickly. She didn't have the heart to tell her mom how many meetings she'd had with the businesspeople in Starling Bay, although thinking about it, that hadn't seemed much like work. Maybe at first, when she had been hesitant and barely knew anyone, but the more she met the various townspeople, the more comfortable she felt.

The longer she stayed and the more she got to know the townspeople, it hadn't felt like work. Life in Starling Bay was relaxed, and everything seemed easier. And the town was pretty. Especially now, around Christmas time. She felt as if she was living in her own little Christmas snow globe.

Meeting Dylan had made her stay here all the more enjoyable. Things had been going well until this evening, but that comment by Rourke had left her with some doubts.

She didn't expect a man like Dylan to be celibate, and she had been surprised and secretly relieved to discover that he wasn't seeing anyone. But Rourke's comment about the dating profile had upset her. She knew it was foolish of her to think anything of it, but like a viral infection, it took hold and spread through her, casting doubts on what they had.

What if Dylan saw her as an easy target? A young woman, well, *young-ish*, not in her prime but not old either. A woman who wasn't sure about herself, about meeting men, or having a relationship; a woman who might be easier to win over than someone who was confident and bold.

She didn't want to be a notch on his bedpost. She colored, the thought making her feel restless. She had only ever been with Brian. The idea of being with someone new frightened her.

In the past she had quickly ended the conversation when her mother or her friends tried to broach the subject of her going 'out there' and meeting someone.

She was content, she told them.

Life was as good as it could be.

And she was happy in her work.

The idea of going out there, as if it were the Wild West, and catching a prize specimen with a lasso, was an anathema.

But Dylan had found a way into her heart.

She had let herself feel vulnerable, had allowed herself to be reeled in. It had happened slowly and naturally, the connection and the attraction, in equal parts, and both making for a heady combination which had been hard to resist.

They had kissed, for goodness' sake. Many times, as it turned out.

And that man gave kisses of the kind that kept her awake at night.

But now she was starting to question him, and his motives, and her vulnerability.

She had moved too fast, and they both knew she was leaving.

The question was, was Dylan Fraser trying to get something from her quickly, or was he a man with nobler intentions?

She wasn't sure. She thought she had come to know the real him, but how well did she really know him?

"Live a little, Meredith," her mother said, getting up slowly. "I'm going to bed."

"Will you be okay to look after Chloe while I'm away?"

"Are you really asking me that question?"

She knew it was a given with her parents. They had always been there for her and they always would be. "Thank you."

"I'm your mother, Meredith. You don't have to thank me for these things." Her mother kissed her gently on the top of her head. "I assume you're driving?" she asked, rolling her eyes.

Her fear of flying, insane and as ridiculous as it seemed, was a real thing. "I'm driving."

"So you'll be gone a few days?"

"If I leave the day after tomorrow, I can stay a few nights and drive back on Christmas Eve, in time for the Christmas pageant."

"Will you be able to do it?" her mother asked, worried. "It's a long drive, honey, and with all the snow."

"I won't have Chloe or Spart. I'll be fine."

CHAPTER 23

*H*e had been busy checking through the props when Chloe's grandparents dropped Chloe off to the rehearsal.

"Your mom must be busy, huh?" Dylan asked Chloe, while adjusting the manger. One of the wooden sides had come loose and the Baby Annabell-Brother Jesus was in danger of falling out.

"She was reading." Chloe held the doll while he hammered in a nail.

"Reading?" He paused, stilling the hammer. Merry wasn't visiting clients, and Hyacinth didn't have her on a wild goose chase running around the town.

She was *reading.*

Chloe's grandparents had dropped her off, and he had a feeling they'd be picking her up as well.

"Reading, huh?" he repeated, not believing that for a moment. He hoped Chloe would reveal some more. The vase Merry had made had been sitting in his workshop, a reminder of her, and that day.

"You fixed it," Chloe stated.

"Yup." He stood back while Chloe put the baby doll back in

the manger. The manger was fixed, but his own personal situation with Merry was anything but fixed. He had a feeling it wouldn't be as simple to fix, either.

"Mom's going back to Boston," Chloe commented, staring at him as if she knew it was news that might interest him.

"Boston? When?"

"Tomorrow morning."

"How come?" He straightened up, trying not to sound too interested, but the way this 'tween was staring back at him told him she knew he was pretending.

"She says it's 'cause of work."

"Work." It was plausible.

"Do you like my Mom?"

This was a level of curiosity he wasn't ready for. "Uh...sure. Your mom's nice."

"Do you like her?" Chloe asked, her eyebrows lifting. This wasn't a conversation he was ready to have with anyone, least of all Meredith's daughter, especially when he himself didn't know how things were or where he stood.

"Your mom is nice." She was more than nice. Merry Nicholls was perfect.

"She works too hard," said Chloe.

"I know."

"She got sick."

"Yes," he replied softly, wondering how hard things must have been for this young girl, first to lose her father, and then to have her mom get sick. "Your mom told me. But she's better now."

"I think you helped her get better."

He bent down so that he was at her level. "I don't think I had much to do with that, Chloe."

"I saw you holding hands the other day."

He raised his eyebrow in surprise. "You did, huh?"

154

Chloe nodded.

"But she's busy reading," he said carefully, "and she's too busy to come here." It would have been nice to see her today. He had called her a few times, but her cell phone had been switched off. He wasn't silly. He knew something had annoyed her that evening at the hotel lobby. Truth was, he knew what had.

"She said she had to do some work stuff."

Christmas Eve was only days away. Was she going to miss the pageant? "How long is she going for?" he asked.

"A couple of days."

He had two more rehearsals planned for this week, and he'd had hopes of seeing Merry at all of them. Now he'd just found out that not only would she not be here, she'd be out of town. Hundreds of miles away in Boston.

It didn't sound good. He needed to find out what was going on.

∾

She wasn't looking forward to the journey, but it would be better than flying. A part of her was loath to leave, but Dan Shepworth had been good to her, and she didn't feel she had a choice in turning him down.

But what lousy timing, given that the pageant was a few days away. Not that she would miss her daughter on the stage, because Chloe didn't have a part and wouldn't be visible, but Chloe was hyped up about working behind the scenes and pitching in. Merry suspected that Dylan had given her a fair share of responsibility and that made her happy.

Watching Chloe blossom in this new place had been eye-opening, and it was what she wanted to see. It wasn't ideal, being away from her daughter in the run-up to Christmas, but she wanted to keep her boss happy. After all, she would be returning to work soon enough, though she didn't have a firm date in mind yet. She tried not to dwell too much on leaving Starling Bay and returning back to her normal life.

"Meredith!" She heard her mother's voice from below. Merry wondered what was up because it wasn't like her mother to yell.

She raced to the landing and peered down. "What's the matt —" But her voice stopped in her throat as she looked at the open door, and at that tall, wide body standing in the doorway. Wearing his bomber jacket as if it were a statement of his masculinity, Dylan looked up at her, his gaze intense and questioning.

"Oh," she said carefully, slowly taking note of her mother's jubilant expression.

"You have a *visitor*," replied her mother, heavy on the emphasis.

He'd turned up on her doorstep and now there was no way of getting out of this. Reluctantly, she descended the stairs. "Thanks, Mom, I've got this." She faced Dylan, her hand on the door as if she needed the support of having something to hold.

"Hey," he said breezily.

"Hi."

"I hear you're going to Boston?" There was a hint of surprise in his voice.

"Don't you want to ask Dylan in?" Her mother's voice behind her grated on her nerves.

"No, Mom," she hissed, turning around and making eyes at her mom. "I've got this." She turned back to Dylan again.

He was about to speak when her mother said, "But it's snowing outside, Meredith."

"Mom!"

"The poor man will catch a chill."

Merry grabbed her coat and hat from the coat stand. "We're going for a walk," she announced, sliding her arms through the coat sleeves.

"We are?" Dylan's face was a picture of surprise as he moved out of the way. Merry brushed past him to leave, then closed the door behind her.

"This is nice," Dylan continued, following her. "It's snowing, and I can't think of anything I'd like to do more than to go for another walk in the snow with you again."

She slipped on her hat and did up her coat buttons.

"This is romantic," he said when she didn't comment.

"It's not meant to be," she retorted, walking at a fast pace. She was eager to get as far away from the house as she could. "I'm trying to get out of my mother's eavesdropping range."

"I like your mom," he countered. "I think she likes me too."

"My mother would like anyone she thought I showed an interest in."

"I feel honored."

She was walking at breakneck speed.

"Slow down, Merry. What's the rush? You're heading towards the town square."

"I know," she said, her voice tight. The truth was, she hadn't been thinking about where she was going. She had hoped to avoid seeing Dylan altogether. It had been the reason she hadn't gone to drop Chloe off at the Fitzsimmons Theater for the rehearsal. And then he'd turned up on her doorstop, forcing her to acknowledge him.

Forcing her to confront things.

She wasn't good at confronting things. She was far better at hunkering down and getting busy.

"Merry," he reached out and grabbed her forearm. "Are you going to tell me what's going on? We're so far away from your house now that your mother can't possibly hear anything unless you're wearing a wire."

She let his attempt at humor slip by. "You don't know my mother."

They stood face-to-face in the street.

"You're going to Boston," he challenged.

"Who told you?"

"Chloe. When were you going to tell me?"

"Since when do I need to tell you anything?"

"You don't, but I'm wondering why you haven't said anything, why you didn't come to drop Chloe off, why you're going to Boston, and why your cell phone is switched off."

She said nothing but looked back at his face, trying to read him. It made her question again as to how well she knew him. How well could she hope to know him? It had been different with Brian. He had been her first real boyfriend—she and Chad Bostwick had never worked out. But Brian, he had been her high-school sweetheart, the boy she had gone to prom with, and who she had ended up marrying. He was the father of her child. Many had said that they had rushed things. A few of her friends had told her she needed to have kissed more frogs, but Brian had been her soulmate, and she had been lost ever since his passing.

Now she had Dylan to contend with and it was a whole new game. She wasn't sure she was playing it too well.

"I'm talking about you and me, and this distance, Merry," he gesticulated with his hands. "This huge gaping hole that's opened up between us."

"I don't know why you're bringing this up."

Snow started to fall around them, and she held out her gloved hands, catching the pretty snowflakes as they fell.

"I don't have a dating profile," he said.

"A what?" she asked, giving a false little laugh. She'd been found out. It was no point trying to deny it, but she was going to, because this was embarrassing. It meant Dylan Fraser could see right through her, and worse, he knew her fears, and thoughts. He had a handle on her feelings.

She didn't want that.

She didn't want anyone to know her as well as that.

It made her vulnerable, and she had spent years building herself up into a woman who was anything but that.

"I don't have a dating profile. Not anymore. It was never my idea in the first place. Rourke instigated it."

"What are you talking about?" She pulled her hat down so that it covered her ears, but more because it made her look as if she wasn't bothered.

"Don't act as if you have no idea what I'm talking about, Merry. Rourke tried to get me to date. He set me up with a profile and tried to make me check out lots of dating sites."

"Why would you think I cared about that?"

"Because I know you. I know how things changed between us, I saw how your smile faded the moment Rourke opened his mouth."

She opened her mouth to deny this claim, but he wasn't finished. "Rourke is a ladies' man. He thinks that most of us are like him. We're not. *I'm* not. We're not so different, you and me, Merry."

It seemed like they were going to have this conversation here. Now. She wasn't ready for it, but he'd done a Dylan on her, made her move outside her comfort zone and forced her to deal with things. Well, she was up for it. "How's that?" She was curious to know. If she was going to get cold and wet and be out as the snowfall seemed to get thicker, she might as well get his take on the situation.

"You're cautious, I sense that. I get it. You don't trust me, or maybe you did, but something changed, and the only reason I can think of why that might be is that one of my best friends opened his mouth and said something stupid. That's the thing about Rourke. He means well, but his take on life is very different than mine. I'm careful about who I let into my life, and I haven't let anyone in for a long time."

She folded her arms.

"Each day I think about how I can casually turn up in town, or wish that you might casually turn up at my store, so that I can see you again."

A tiny breath escaped from her lungs. *He did?*

"Each time it's rehearsal day, I look forward to seeing you, and I've never looked forward to having rehearsals as much as I do now, ever since you came along."

"I was busy today," she said, coughing. "Busy reading."

"Reading? Or avoiding me? Because if you've been avoiding me, I wish you'd come out and say whatever it is that you're avoiding me for. I wish you'd stop hiding behind your silence and say what you feel."

"Say what I feel?" she asked, not used to dealing with these things. Affairs of the heart, and all that other stuff. "What do *you* feel?" she asked, curious.

"That's easy. I feel happier when you're around. I *like* having you around, Merry. I'm not a guy who's on the lookout for women. Sure, I've had my share of heartache. I've had my heart broken, and I know you've experienced the greatest heartache. We don't even know that much about one another because we never seem to find the time to sit down and talk about these things properly, even though I find myself wondering what it would be like to have a meal with you, to take you out one evening and have you to myself for more than a few snatched moments here and there. If you knew me, you would understand that I, too, am wary of meeting someone. I'm not Rourke, and I'm not Reed. I don't have it so lucky in that department. I'm cautious, and slow, and prone to hiding my feelings—but then you came along, and all of my reservations fell to the side."

She would have taken a step back, had his words not rooted her to the cold ground.

She wanted to believe him.

Wanted to, and she considered his words, but then something inside her snapped—like an elastic band stretched beyond its limit. The reverberations bounced around her head, as if his words were too much to take in.

She'd only stepped out to get away from her mother's prying ears. She hadn't expected him to prise her open, look inside and find all her insecurities.

"Don't walk away, Merry. Don't," he said, as she turned to leave. He advanced towards her. "I know you're protecting yourself. I get it, Merry. I know how it must seem to you, seeing me and my friends sitting around and having a couple of beers, and then Rourke making a stupid comment that probably scared you off and set off all these alarm bells in your head."

She tried to make light of it, because he'd hit the nail on the head and gotten to the bullseye of her insecurities. "I'm not upset that you've been on the online dating circuit."

"Aren't you?"

"No. What you did before is your business. I'm not expecting you to be a saint."

"Then why did you retreat?"

Because she felt inadequate. Because she was suddenly fearful that the guy she had started to have feelings for might be a lothario. That he might not be the kind of guy she thought him to be, but someone else; a player, and she wasn't a chess piece on a chess board of life, nor did she have the moves and countermoves to deal with him.

She had only ever been with one man and it had been so long ago since she had felt this way about anyone. She hadn't had a conversation like this for a long, long time, and she felt out of practice, out of touch. Kissing him had been a mistake, for it had led her to believe in the magic of romance again, but there was so much at stake now, at this age, and with her responsibilities; with Chloe, and her work and her life back in

Boston. It wasn't as simple as finding someone and falling in love.

Work was so much easier to contend with.

Suddenly, Boston, Dan Shepworth, and the board meeting seemed more appealing.

But Dylan was calling her out on it. He had somehow encroached on her private space and was trying to take up residence.

Only, she wasn't ready for it.

"Why, Merry? Why are you putting up your defenses? Why not take a chance on me?"

"I've been in the dating game," she said, lifting her face and staring back at him defiantly, hoping he wouldn't see through her.

"You have, have you?" He sounded as if he didn't believe her.

"I've kissed my share of frogs."

"You have?" he asked, his voice suddenly gentle and sweet, like honey. She stared back at him, at that tiny dimple that always drew her gaze. "Yes," she lied, her heart starting to race. He looked like a movie star, with his big build, and strong shoulders. When she'd discovered he was an artist, it had surprised her. At times he was like two different men, soft and gentle, yet quietly strong.

His gaze locked onto her, making it impossible for her to look away, and in her head, she silently contemplated reasoning and logic, as if these things would protect her.

He moved towards her. "Any of them kiss you like I did?"

How could she not look at his lips now? How could she not think about wanting more? She knew what it felt like, having those arms around her and his soft lips on hers. Her heart was thundering, getting ready to explode, and if she stood out here any longer, gazing at this man who was her kryptonite, she would soon give in.

She wasn't supposed to give in.

She was supposed to be getting ready to leave for Boston, and start thinking about her return to her normal life in a few weeks' time. She couldn't allow herself to think about Dylan.

The snow began to fall faster and thicker. Soft, chunky flakes floated down like weighted feathers. It was eerily silent. In the distance she could see the huge Christmas tree all lit up in the center of the town square.

She was in her own perfect Christmas card setting, with a man who until yesterday might have been the closest she had ever come to trusting, besides Brian. But doubts had surfaced. It wasn't only Rourke opening her eyes to another side of Dylan. She'd started to wonder what this could possibly lead to.

She had become caught up in the fairytale, seeing all the good parts, and forgetting that the man was only human, and therefore would have his fair share of faults.

"You haven't answered my question, Merry."

"I don't think this is a good idea," she said finally.

He tilted his head as if he hadn't heard right. "Why? What's the worst that could happen?"

The worst that could happen? She could get her heart broken; open herself up to something which would hurt her. Why would she do that when life was pretty good as it was?

"I leave for Boston tomorrow," she said, looking away. "And then we'll go back for good after the New Year." It would be insane, not to mention spontaneous and therefore not carefully thought out, if she let Dylan kiss her now.

She reminded herself that she wasn't that type of woman. She was hard-working, focused and sensible. These were the traits which had gotten her through life after Brian. She still had a ways to go, and things to do; issues to fix, not least of all her relationship with Chloe.

Looking for love was not on her list of priorities.

"I understand," he said. It was only the tiny little twitch in his

163

jaw which told her that all might not be well under that smooth, unruffled exterior of his. "Whatever you say, Merry."

She pressed her lips together. He looked like a wounded animal, trying to appear brave. And that was when she understood who he was. He'd been right there in front of her...big, and brave and looking like a man who could take anything life dealt, but deep down, he was a man with feelings, and soul, and the ability to absorb pain.

"You're getting wet," he said, and he almost reached out to touch her hat, but instead ended up rubbing his gloved hands together. "We should get back."

CHAPTER 24

*R*eed walked into the store, surprising him. "What brings you here?" Dylan asked. "Looking for Christmas presents?"

"Unless you sell diamonds, no."

"Is that all Olivia wants?" Dylan asked, smiling.

"Isn't it obvious?"

"It's good that you got her a three carat diamond engagement ring, then." Dylan rearranged the display of the new snow globes that had come in this morning.

"Two carat," said Reed, picking one up, then turning the wind up key at the bottom. The globe emitted a tinny tune.

"Two carat, three carat," mused Dylan. "It's a huge rock whichever way you look at it."

"Pretty," Reed remarked, staring at the globe and ignoring Dylan's comment.

Dylan started to tidy the mess of empty boxes. "Are you on your way to the Heights?" The new luxury development had a good chunk of Reed's money behind it and now that the apartments were going up for sale, it wasn't uncommon for his friend to drop by from time to time.

"I came to see you, actually."

Dylan turned around. "Something wrong?"

"Does something have to be wrong for me to come and see you?"

"No...but..." He examined his friend's face for a clue. Reed looked tired, that was all. He often did, staying up late at night, taking care of his many businesses.

"How's it going with your marketing expert?"

"She's gone back to Boston. Said she had some work stuff to sort out."

"For how long?"

"She'll be back in time for the pageant."

Reed's eyes twinkled with a hint of mischief. "Anything you want to tell me?"

"Nothing in particular."

"Why do I get the feeling you're holding something back? You don't trust your friends anymore?"

"I'm not sure I have anything to tell you," Dylan replied truthfully.

"Strange," said Reed pensively. He scratched his chin. "I got the vibe that there was something going on between you both the other night."

"She's not...we're not....it's not..." He struggled to explain. How was he supposed to know what they were?

"Sounds complicated."

"It shouldn't be," mumbled Dylan.

"Oh?"

He wasn't about to spill his heart out to Reed, but Merry had said she didn't want to take things further, and what could he say to that? He understood her, at least, he thought he did. He sensed it was a combination of things, her starting to trust again, and needing to be extra careful, given that she had responsibility in the form of Chloe. Maybe it was too much for her to take on. Also, Rourke hadn't helped.

"Did Rourke put his foot in it?" Reed asked.

"When does that guy not put his foot in it? Anyway, you didn't come out here to give me relationship advice," noted Dylan. "Not that we have a relationship," he added quickly.

"No, I didn't. I came to see how you were." Reed patted him on the back. "I like her. I don't know her, but I like her. She seems to have caught your attention, and that has to count for something."

Dylan breathed in loud and hard, thinking about it.

"I'd hate to think your last girlfriend put you off women forever."

"She almost did, but I'm over her now."

"I'm hoping Meredith can change that for you. Here," Reed handed him a shiny card.

"What's this?" Dylan asked, glancing at the embossed gold-colored writing. It was an invite.

"A New Year's Eve party invite."

"Classy," he drawled, impressed. "Olivia's influence?"

"Who else?"

"She's a classy lady," replied Dylan chivalrously. "I'd expect nothing less."

"If it was left to me, I'd go for a few drinks at the Blue Velvet Bar, but she's insisting on having a big party."

"And why not?" Dylan wondered if he could get Merry to come, and then, in the blink of an eye, he remembered that there was no point in making plans like that.

Reed pinched the bridge of his nose and let out a sigh. "She's always having parties. Sometimes it gets a bit too much. But, well, we're doing this so…try and come."

"Thanks," he said. "I'll be there."

"Bring a friend," said Reed, punching him gently in the stomach.

"I should be able to find one," he said, grinning. He hoped that Merry would at least stay until New Year's. If she did, he would ask her.

"Do you want to go for a beer later?" Reed suggested.

"Not tonight. We've got rehearsals back to back."

"I'd forgotten, Mr. Spielberg." Reed laughed. "Do we have front-row seats to this extravaganza?"

"VIP seats all the way." Reed knew the layout; a few rows of chairs set out in the town square with people standing around the edges. "Don't laugh too hard if Baby Jesus falls out of the crib."

"Hard not to."

He had another rehearsal later that evening. No sooner had he arrived, than he wished it was over and done with.

"Did your mom get there okay?" he asked Chloe when she came in. She nodded. "She left really early yesterday."

"It's a long drive. It must have taken her a long time."

"Mom hates flying."

"She does?" He'd always assumed it was because of the beast that she'd had to drive.

"After dad…"

"Oh." Of course. It made sense. "Sorry, Chloe."

The girl shrugged. "Grandma says she'll grow out of it one day."

He was about to say something when Chloe's grandmother suddenly appeared. He recognized her instantly from the other day. "Irene Hawkins." The woman held out her hand.

"Nice to see you again, Mrs. Hawkins."

"We're excited to see the performance."

"It should be a good one," he agreed, crossing his arms over his chest. "You do know that Chloe isn't in the actual performance?"

"We know. She's already warned us. She'll be backstage."

"There isn't much of a stage either," he said, feeling the need to make excuses. Merry's family wasn't from Starling Bay and he assumed that they wouldn't be familiar with the Christmas pageants they had here. He didn't know what they did in Boston, but he felt the need to manage people's expectations. "It's out in the open, I'm afraid. But the town square is packed on Christmas Eve, and we have a section in one corner. It tends to be buffered from the cold."

"No matter what the weather, I assure you that we'll be there," Merry's mother said. She grinned. "Even if it is to watch Chloe behind the scenes."

"I hope so." It was almost on the tip of his tongue to ask about Merry, but he somehow managed to hold off. He was certain that she wouldn't like that, him prying into her business. Her leaving home the other day and having a conversation with him out of her mother's earshot had confirmed that for him.

"Meredith is hoping to be back in time."

"Chloe was saying," he replied carefully.

"She's going to set off early on Christmas Eve morning, and I expect she'll be here by noon. I have a feeling she'll be eager to be back in Starling Bay early."

At least that was something. "The show starts at 7:00 p.m. and it only lasts about half an hour."

"We look forward to it," she said, giving him a bright smile. She looked as if she was about to walk away, but instead, she touched his arm. "This is all new for Meredith. I don't like to interfere, but you need to give her some time."

He looked surprised, and was momentarily speechless.

"She hasn't let anyone in, not after Brian. We were worried

that she might never, but she seems happier and more relaxed these days."

He wasn't sure what she was talking about. If Merry was happier and more relaxed, he doubted that it was because of him.

"Give her time."

"Give her time?" he asked, echoing her words.

She nodded. "My husband's waiting downstairs with Spartacus," she said, retreating. "We're going to take him for a walk while you actors act."

CHAPTER 25

"It's great to have you back, Meredith. We've missed you." Dan Shepworth walked into his office where Merry had been waiting for him while he took a call in another office.

Two hours she'd been sitting in the conference room, in a meeting with her boss and other department managers, looking over how things had fared at the store this year and firming up plans for the coming year.

Now that it was only the two of them, there was a pregnant pause in which Merry got the feeling that he expected her to say the same—that she had missed being at work. Only, she hadn't missed any of it; not the work, or Boston.

She smiled, instead.

"It's good to be back," she replied.

But it wasn't. Her house had been cold and dusty, and with no Chloe and Spartacus to fill it, it hadn't been exactly cozy. It had been nice enough, coming back, but it felt odd—as if she was a guest returning to her not-so-great hotel room after spending the night in a luxury penthouse suite. It was the closest she could come to describing how it felt to return to Boston and to leave Starling Bay behind.

She had arrived yesterday afternoon, after a grueling six-hour drive. Thankfully, with Chloe and Spartacus not being with her, she hadn't had to stop off every hour for a break. But the weather had been atrocious, and she'd had to drive carefully. When she arrived home, she needed some sort of comfort, and so she had indulged herself by taking a long bubble bath.

"How are you doing?" He sat down in his thick leather chair, and leaned back, clasping his hands over his large stomach.

"Very well," she replied, nodding. "Very well."

"It must be boring, sitting around doing nothing all day?"

"I haven't had time to do much of that."

Dan's thick eyebrows pushed together. "I hope you'll come back invigorated. We have a lot of work to do for next year." He sounded like his usual enthusiastic, go-getting self. She had often become wrapped up in his visions of more, more, more. Chasing more sales, always on the lookout for ways to get more customers in the store. She had thrived on the thrill of wanting to excel.

"I can imagine." The thought of all that work, those long, long hours, and meeting after meeting—it suddenly didn't appeal. She sat back in her chair and put down her pen.

A couple of times during the boring-as-hell meeting, she had drifted off, her mind and thoughts back in Starling Bay, recalling the walk in the woods with Dylan, the snow, the openness of the countryside. Each time she thought of Dylan, it made her heart jolt. She told herself that absence made the heart grow fonder, then reprimanded herself for having that thought in the first place.

But try as she did, she couldn't stop herself from thinking about him. She had been caught off guard when Shepworth asked her to go over the figures for the third quarter of the year and explain the dip in sales. It had been a wrench to pull herself away from Roxy's, and the town square, and The Grand Hotel, and stare at her spreadsheet trying to remember what the issue had been. Luckily, she knew her numbers and she hadn't even had to refer to the paperwork to tell them what had gone wrong.

"Kate isn't bad, but she's not *you*." Dan was silent then, and she knew he was waiting to hear what her plans were; that he wanted to know when she would return.

"I'll spend some time with her today, looking over things," she replied.

"I expect she'll need to hand over the reins soon?"

He was eager, no doubt, for her to return. She had only been away for a month, and her doctor had signed her off for two months. She thought of Starling Bay, of its charming row of shops and houses overlooking the sea, and the seafront, of the town square with its Christmas tree and lights, and how she could walk from her house to the Fitzsimmons Theater and then to Fellini's or The Grand Hotel. She thought of Dylan's store and his workshop, and the day he'd taught her to make a vase. The way his hands had guided her, the way his fingers had touched hers. It had been a tender and intimate moment.

"What's so funny?"

She looked up at her boss.

"You're smiling," he said.

"I...uh...was I?" She clasped her hands together, executive style. "I still have a month's sick leave left, Dan."

"That's right. So you do." He coughed lightly. "We're going to have a good year next year, Meredith. It's going to be busy for sure."

She forced a laugh. "When is it never busy here?"

"That's why we love it, don't we?" He laughed.

She had made her point, and he hadn't pressed. She had a month, and she had decided she would spend it in Starling Bay. If anyone had asked her what her plans were twenty-four hours ago, before she'd left Starling Bay, she'd have said it was to return to

Boston. Not to work, but back to the city. She had envisaged yoga classes, and lunch and coffee with friends.

But stepping foot inside her house changed all of that. Even the way she felt about that last conversation with Dylan changed. Being away from him had made her see things from a different perspective.

"Next month?" he asked.

"Yes."

Because she knew him so well, she could see the tell-tale tightening around his lips. He didn't like her answer. "I suppose we can last without you for another month."

"The rest has done me good."

"It has. You look well."

"Thank you." Her colleagues in her team had said the same. She certainly felt better.

"Are you set for tomorrow?"

The board meeting was starting in mid-morning, and she had a whole day to prepare for it. Between her and Kate, it wouldn't be as difficult.

"I'm set."

"Good." He sat forward and clasped his hands together. "And don't forget tomorrow evening, 8:00 p.m. sharp."

How could she forget? She was less fazed about the presentation to the board members than she was about the annual cocktail-and-canapés at Shepworth's house. She had attended every year, except for the year that Brian had passed away, and the year she'd had Chloe.

"Another year, another party," she said, something heavy settling in her stomach. She usually tolerated these things, and only because it was work-related, but this time she was filled with dread. The thought of sitting in Dan's sprawling mansion talking to the board members and other department managers did not appeal. But she had no excuse this year. She was back in Boston, and even though it wasn't something she wanted to attend, she felt as if she had no choice. "I'm looking forward to it," she said, forcing a smile.

"Good."

She left his office and set to work, eager to get the day over and done with. Because she was so busy, time flew. There was much to do, graphs and data to pull together into an easy-to-see format.

She spent the rest of the day with Kate, who brought her up to date with things that had gone on, and had gone wrong, while she had been away. And after that, they worked together on tomorrow's presentation.

She left the office earlier than she had ever done, given that there was such an important meeting tomorrow. Whether it was because Kate was here, and she was able to delegate more of the work, or whether it was because she had been away and wasn't as caught up with things at the office, but she found herself slacking. Not being unduly careless with her work, but not caring as much.

Her focus had shifted, and all she could think about was Chloe and Starling Bay. But returning home served only to increase her sense of restlessness. The place was empty without Chloe and Spartacus. Spart would have bounded around as soon as she walked through the door. She thought about Chloe who would often be ready for bed by the time she got home late many times in the week, and of her parents who would be getting ready to leave when she returned home.

She called home and her mother answered. After asking her how she was, Merry asked to speak to Chloe.

"She's at the rehearsal. It's the last one," her mother told her.

"The last one?" Merry instantly imagined Dylan at the Fitzsimmons Theater, with Leah Shriver having him all to herself. A shard of jealousy pricked her. "How come's it's the last one?"

"Dylan says the children need a rest day tomorrow."

There would be no rehearsal tomorrow, which was good. They'd had quite a few rehearsals this week and she imagined that Chloe was tired.

"How are you? Your boss and colleagues must be pleased to have you back for a while."

"Dan was asking me when I'd be coming back."

"I bet he was," her mother replied dryly.

"I think he wanted me to say I'd return soon after the holidays."

"What did you say?"

"That I had another month left."

"Well, that's new coming from you."

"I don't know what you mean," Merry protested.

"You must be missing Starling Bay."

"I miss my daughter."

"And the dog. Don't forget your dog."

"I miss you too, Mom."

"I spoke to your young man the other day."

"He's not mine, Mom, and I doubt if he's that young."

"He's thirty-five."

"You didn't ask him!" Merry gasped, before pinching the bridge of her nose. Goodness. She could imagine her mother wandering around Starling Bay hunting down single men in their thirties.

"I asked that other lady, Leah."

Merry was mortified. "What did you go and ask her for?"

"For my dossier."

"Mom!"

"I was very discreet, and that woman loves to talk."

"What else did you say?"

"Nothing."

She needed to return quickly. "Please don't embarrass me," she pleaded. "Don't go asking anyone for anything."

"I won't."

"Tell Chloe I'll call her tomorrow."

She hung up, feeling a little happier at hearing about the goings-on in Starling Bay. She was sorry to have missed Chloe, and imagined her at the Fitzsimmons Theater. And then she thought of Dylan.

She had the sudden urge to hear his voice again. Twice she almost called him, and twice she stopped short because she knew he'd be leading the rehearsal. Sitting alone in her living room eating a sandwich in front of the TV, she imagined Dylan's soft voice and that easygoing laugh of his. But what would she say to him? She had to be sure of her feelings for him, and what they might mean. It was easy enough to romanticize her emotions for Dylan, sitting in the cold loneliness of her life in Boston. But was being with him even possible?

How would it work with her in Boston and him in Starling Bay?

She would have to see how she felt about him when she saw him at the pageant. It would only be two more nights before she was back in Starling Bay.

CHAPTER 26

"That went well," said Dan when the conference room had emptied. He was obviously pleased with her presentation. She had to admit it had gone exceedingly well.

"Thank you. Kate helped," she offered, eager not to hog all the accolade.

"Yes, I'm sure she did."

"She did," Merry insisted, watching Kate pack away the laptop. "She's good." She didn't understand why Dan had issues.

"Nonetheless, it will be good to have you back heading the team, Meredith."

It seemed his issue was that he wanted Merry back. He wanted long hours, and an employee who never said 'no' to any task.

Unfortunately, she wasn't that employee any more.

Merry smiled at him, but said nothing.

"Eight o'clock tonight," Dan reminded her.

"I haven't forgotten."

She walked back to her desk, which was across from Kate's. "That went well, don't you think?" asked Merry.

"It did. You're really good." There was a hint of envy in her voice. "You're so confident in your delivery."

"Thank you," beamed Merry. She was in her element at work, and standing up in a room full of people wasn't difficult. A memory floated back to her of the town hall meeting, and that night when Hyacinth had called her up on stage, and how seeing Dylan in the crowd had thrown her off.

"I wish I could be that good."

"You can. It takes practice, that's all. I wasn't always like that, and I've had plenty of practice. You should have presented it." She'd given Kate the chance to, but Kate had turned it down. Merry wasn't sure how Dan would have received it, Kate giving the presentation in lieu of Merry, but it would have been interesting to see his reaction, at the very least. "Maybe you can try next time?" she suggested.

"Next time?" Kate asked. "You're back soon, aren't you?"

"Not for another month."

"That's not what Dan said."

"What did Dan say?" She was most intrigued to hear.

Kate shrugged. "He seems to think you'll be back after the holidays."

Merry shook her head slowly. "I have some more time to take off."

"Are you okay now?" Kate asked, her face turning serious. "You look okay."

"I'm fine." She remembered the presentation to the management team, months ago, where she had messed up badly. She had clammed up, unable to continue. Maybe it hadn't had anything to do with Brian, or the five-year anniversary? Maybe the almost-breakdown had been an indication of her burnout?

She not only felt relaxed and somewhat detached from the goings-on at Boyd & Meyer, she was getting anxious about returning to Starling Bay.

"Do you want anything?" Kate asked, slipping her coat on.

"I'm getting a coffee."

"No, thanks."

She waited until Kate had left, then called home, suddenly longing to hear Chloe's voice.

"Hey, sweetie," she squealed, her voice softening at the sound of Chloe's excited voice.

"Hey, Mom."

"How are you? How's the pageant coming along?"

"It's coming along real good!"

"Are you ready?"

"Yup! Dylan's put me in charge of the lighting." In the background she heard Spartacus barking, and her mother issuing orders to her father.

"There's going to be lighting?" She had no idea what type of stage area there would be, but she had prepared herself for the bare minimum. Lighting hadn't even factored into it.

"You'll see. We have some cool special effects."

"Special effects?" She really had imagined a minimalistic stage area. "I can't wait."

"When are you coming back?"

"Tomorrow."

"But we're doing the show tomorrow."

"I know. I'm going to leave first thing in the morning, and I will be there by late afternoon."

"The show starts at 7:00 p.m."

"I know, Chloe."

"Dylan said the town square starts to get busy from 5:00 p.m. onwards, so he said to come early, so that you get a good place in the front."

"I'll be back before then."

"But can we go early? There are a lot of stalls and Grandpa gave me some money so that I can buy presents."

"On Christmas Eve?" she asked, laughing. "Aren't you

leaving it a bit late?"

"I told you we needed to go shopping last weekend, but you were busy with Miss Fitzsimmons."

Merry lowered her head, remembering. "I'm sorry. I'm going to get there really early tomorrow, okay?"

"Promise?"

"I promise."

"Dylan was asking when you'd be back."

There was something odd about Chloe's voice when she made that statement, and Merry couldn't figure out if she was teasing or curious, or if she had dropped that sliver of information on purpose. "You can tell him now, can't you?"

Her daughter laughed. "He likes you, Mom."

She didn't know how to respond to that. "Oh, I think he likes most people."

"But he likes you the most."

"I don't know about that."

"Grandma says he likes you. She was talking to him the other day."

"Your Grandma," wailed Merry. "I don't know what I'm going to do with her." She inwardly cringed at the idea of her mother eliciting information out of Dylan. It was probably better she came sooner in order to keep her mother at bay.

"Chloe!" Merry heard her mother's voice.

"Grandma's calling me, Mom. I gotta go."

"I'll see you tomorrow, honey."

Merry hung up and considered her options.

What's the worst that could happen?

Dylan's voice swam around in her head.

What's the worst that could happen if she missed the party? Or drove home tonight? Or switched jobs?

No. Too far. Too fast.

What was the worst that could happen—if she allowed herself to follow her heart?

She was still thinking things over a few hours later when she went to the washroom to touch up her makeup.

"Ready for the party?" Kate asked as she sprayed perfume on her wrists.

"I suppose so," Merry replied, getting her lipstick out of her bag. The plan was to meet for drinks at the bar near work, and then to Uber it in groups to Shepworth's mansion. Nobody wanted to turn up alone. As well as managers and board members, he usually invited a few of his socialite friends. It wasn't exactly a *fun* night, but she went because it was the thing to do, because if you had any sense and any career aspirations, you didn't miss out on such a night.

"I'll be at my desk waiting," said Kate.

"I'll be out in a moment."

"I'll wait for you."

Only, as she watched a couple of the other women brush their hair, and add more concealer, she looked at herself and suddenly didn't want to go to any trouble to redo her face in order to go to a dinner party she didn't particularly want to go to, with people she didn't have much to say to. A glance at her watch told her that she could ditch this and leave tonight. She was nuts to drive home first thing tomorrow morning. What was the point in turning up in the afternoon, tired from driving, and having missed most of Christmas Eve which was, for her, the most magical part of Christmas?

"You haven't touched up your lipstick," Kate informed her.

"I've had a change of heart. I'm going to skip the party."

"You're not coming?" Kate blinked, her long, stiff eyelashes heavy with mascara. "Why not?"

"I'm going home."

"To get changed?"

"I'm going back to Starling Bay. Chloe's been working on a

Christmas pageant and I don't want to miss it."

Kate blinked furiously fast, as if she was having problems processing this piece of news. "A Christmas pageant?" The event had no meaning for her. "But what about Shepworth's party?"

"I'm sure you'll have lots of fun."

"Don't you want to come at all?" Kate pressed. "Not even for an hour?"

"I've got a long drive ahead of me. I want to leave as soon as possible." Tonight, she'd rush back, grab her things, and leave. She didn't have much to pack, and if she left now, she would arrive home by midnight. "And I want to surprise my daughter."

"Okay," said Kate, brushing the matter off as if it was of little consequence to her. "I'll see you next year, won't I?" She walked over, and kissed Merry on both cheeks.

"Yes, you will."

"What shall I tell Mr. Shepworth?"

"Tell him Merry said what's the worst that can happen?"

"What?" Kate looked at her as if a Martian had just landed on her head.

"Have a good Christmas," Merry told her.

She watched the gaggle of women leaving the office. An assortment of aromas, from the pungent smell of too much perfume to the sharp scent of hairspray, lingered in the air long after they had gone.

Merry looked around at her computer, and her desk, and moved two stray pens on the table into the desk organizer.

Starling Bay wasn't home, but neither was this office, and neither, as she had lain in bed last night trying to fall asleep, was her home in the suburbs.

Home was where Chloe was, and Spartacus was, and their cozy little home was. Even if, technically, it didn't belong to them.

Home was where the people you loved and cared about were.

CHAPTER 27

*T*he snow was falling by the time she left, but it was light and fluffy, the type that drifted easily in the wind. She switched on the radio and settled back in her seat, her eyes on the dark road stretching out in front of her while Christmas songs filled her car.

It was just over three hundred miles, and she was determined to do it without a single stop along the way. It would have been easier to make this journey in the daylight, but leaving now meant she would be home by the time Chloe woke up on Christmas Eve morning.

She was going to do it, no matter what.

The first hundred miles was easy enough. She blasted the radio which helped. She started yawning towards the end of hitting two hundred miles, but she told herself that she was on the last stretch home. She reminded herself that she was nearer to Starling Bay than she was Boston, and mentally, this gave her an edge.

She perked up, inserted another Christmas CD that Chloe loved listening to, and continued on her journey. By this time, the snow was falling thick and fast, and settling on the ground.

It was darker on these roads, and, finding herself growing increasingly tired, she stopped off at the next gas station to refuel. She also got herself a strong cup of coffee, a bottle of water and some chocolate.

Chocolate made everything seem better. Placing her coffee cup in the cup holder, she got ready to set off again. Only the Jeep didn't start.

"Oh, no," she murmured, turning the key again. When it didn't start a second time, she began to worry. "Please," she begged, as if her Jeep could hear her and respond. Why hadn't she let Dylan take a look at it when he'd asked? He might have been able to fix it.

"No," she pleaded again, desperate to reach home. "*Please*." She prayed silently and turned the key again, and this time the Jeep spluttered to life. She exhaled the breath she'd been holding in, and relaxed her shoulders, smiling with glee.

Feeling happy and relieved, she drove off, imagining the surprise on everyone's faces when they woke up. She planned to get up early and make pancakes for breakfast, filling the house with that lovely, buttery smell. She couldn't wait to see Chloe's face.

Lost in her own thoughts, she drove on, but the snow was getting dangerously thick as it fell in chunks. She turned down the radio, and focused on the road ahead. When her phone rang, she glanced at it quickly, and saw that it was Chloe calling.

She didn't dare answer; the snow was beginning to set, and she needed to concentrate, but when Chloe called a second time, she pulled over to the side of the road, worried. "Chloe, what's wrong?" Her heart was in her mouth, especially when she realized she had six missed calls from her daughter. She'd been blasting the music and hadn't heard any of the calls.

"Mom, don't forget my Christmas sweater."

Merry sat back, relief washing over her. "Is that why you called?" *For the Christmas sweater?*

Six times.

"Don't forget it, Mom. Pleeeeease. I want to wear it at the show."

It was obviously too late, and she was banking on her own early appearance making up for her not bringing the Christmas sweater. "Okay, but," she glanced at the time on the cell phone, it was eleven o'clock. "It's late. Shouldn't you be asleep?"

"I'm going now."

"Goodnight, honey."

She hung up, and looked out of the window. Snow was falling heavily, and she was thankful to be in the warmth of her Jeep. With the engine idling away, she sat back and ground out a long sigh, feeling suddenly tired, now that she had stopped for a moment. Focusing on the road ahead, driving in this weather at this time of night was tiring. She couldn't stop herself from yawning, and picked up her coffee cup to take a long sip. The strong coffee kickstarted her senses, but the chill in the air was starting to bite. She turned up the heater, but it only made her more sleepy.

She would be home in a few hours' time. The welcome thought spurred her into action, and she was determined to get a move on. Setting the coffee cup back down, she set off again, but she had barely gone more than a few yards when the engine spluttered, then died.

"*No!*" she moaned, and turned the key frantically. She tried the ignition again. But the engine didn't start.

"Come on," she cooed, "you can do it. Come on." As soon as she got back, she would take the Jeep to the garage and get it fixed. Forcing herself to remain calm, she tried the engine a few times, and once or twice it spluttered to life, giving her heart reason to soar, but then it died just as quickly.

Panic gripped her chest. "Come on. Come on. Come on," she pleaded, but the car was as dead as a dodo. She looked around at the all-encompassing darkness, with only the soft illumination of her car headlights on the snow.

She turned the key so that everything was off, including the headlights. Maybe the battery needed to get some charge back, she reasoned. She could only hope, not knowing much about cars, and wishing she could go back in time and have Dylan look it over.

But now she was in near darkness. Now she was suddenly afraid. She tried to remember which way she'd come, tried hard to gauge her bearings. After leaving the gas station, she'd taken a turn towards Springfield. That's right, *Springfield*. She willed herself not to panic, to stay calm, but her breath burst in and out, her lungs the only part of her capable of moving. She felt frozen to the spot, her limbs locking up in fright.

She must have only sat with the car switched off for a few moments, but the snow had fallen so fast that her windshield was blanketed completely and she couldn't see a thing.

The fear was starting to rise, and she was suddenly afraid. She turned the ignition, and yet again, the engine showed no signs of coming to life. She turned the windshield wipers on, and put the headlights on again, relieved to see the snow being wiped away, and the light once more in front of her.

She had to act and fast, and she tried desperately to remember the name of the roadside assistance service. When she looked at her phone, her battery was down to ten percent. Her heart sank as she remembered she'd left her charger still plugged into the socket back in her apartment.

She tried to remain calm, tried to practice her breathing, tried not to wail in despair. She picked up the phone and found the number of the roadside assistance company, but her instinct told her that by the time the operator took all her details for verification, her phone might die completely.

What could she do?

Dylan.

She could call Dylan.

He would know what to do.

If it was a simple thing like...like...not enough water in the ....in some part of the system, Dylan could talk her through it. And she had water. If it was something as simple as that, Dylan would know and she could fix it, and she would be on her way.

That's what she would do. Call Dylan.

Only, when she found his number and hit the DIAL button, the signal strength bar went to zero.

She'd had a signal just a few moments ago.

In despair, she stared at her phone, waiting, waiting, waiting for the signal bar to reappear. And when, after a few moments it didn't, her hopes plummeted further. She couldn't sit here waiting for it when time wasn't on her side.

She had to get out and walk around until she got a signal. It was all she could do, before her phone battery died completely and she had no chance at all.

She didn't want to get out of the car. It was so deathly quiet around here. Why couldn't she have broken down at the gas station? Why here, in the middle of nowhere, in almost total darkness?

She waited for her courage to build, and pulled the collar of the coat around her neck. She rubbed her hands together, then pulled out her woolen hat from her bag and put it on. The temperatures seemed to have dropped further, and she was starting to feel it.

She wasn't going to call roadside assistance. She was going to call Dylan, but before she ventured outside, she needed a flashlight. Sliding her fingers along the lock of the glove compartment, it took three tries before she managed to open it. Her hands were so cold now, but she grabbed the flashlight, switched it on to check that it was working, and then sat in the car, trying to pluck up the courage to leave the car. Adrenaline spiked inside her, making her feel jittery. She had to do it. She had to do it now. She flung the car door open, still sitting in the driver's seat. The burst of light from her flashlight lit up the snow-carpeted ground, providing small comfort. At least it wasn't totally dark now, but it was eerily silent. For a moment, it reminded her of the night in the town square with Dylan.

She shook her head, dismissing the thought, then pointed the flashlight all around, on the alert for danger, or trouble, or moving figures.

Or a serial killer.

Her mind conjured up a montage of her worst fears.

She strode out, closing the car door behind her, and holding her cell phone in the other hand. She lifted it high into the air, and prayed as she walked around, willing for the signal strength bars to appear. And when they did, she called him quickly, her heart thundering like whitewater rapids. She prayed he would answer it quickly, and he did. He answered on the second ring. Impressive, given that it was so late.

"Merry?"

"I'm in trouble," she cried, shining her flashlight around like a weapon of defense. "My car's not starting—"

"Where are you?"

"In a pull-off area, I came off the highway. I've been driving for four hours, and I don't have much battery life left on my phone and—"

"Where exactly are you?"

"Springfield, I think. I'm a hundred miles from home. From Starling Bay, I mean."

"I know where you are." His voice was calm, yet forceful.

"I left a gas station and turned left towards Springfield, and then about twenty minutes out, my car died."

"Can you call roadside assistance?"

"My battery is about to die, and I don't have a charger cable. I'm scared, Dylan." She flinched, thinking she'd heard something, then looked around quickly. It was nothing.

"Don't be. I'm coming to get you."

But he would be a while. She couldn't stay here. She couldn't. "I can look under the hood. Should I look under the hood?"

But he appeared not to be listening. "Why did you leave tonight, Merry? The weather's so bad. Didn't you check before you took off?"

Spoken like a typical man. She ground her teeth together. "I called you to see if you could help me, not to have you lecture me on the state of the weather."

"I'm sorry, that's not what I meant. I just want you to be saf—"

The phone went dead. "Dylan?" she cried. Her heart felt as if it was going to sprint right out of her chest. Frantic, she stabbed at her phone to check what had died, the battery or the signal. "Dylan?"

Crunch.

Swoosh.

She heard something behind her, and the hairs at the back of her neck stood up. It was soft, barely a rustle. It was the sound of footsteps nearby.

Her breath seized up for one terrifying moment and she spun around with her flashlight. Something rushed past behind the trees. She screamed, and dropped her phone and the flashlight, and raced towards the car. She yanked the door open and dove in, locking the doors quickly. Sinking back in the seat, she slid down lower and lower, not daring to look out. Waiting, waiting, waiting.

Anticipating '*it*'.

She was shaking all over, her teeth chattering, only it wasn't from the cold. Involuntary little seizures gripped her muscles. She had never been this frightened before in her entire life.

It must have been a while before things evened out; her heart rate and pulse, and that roaring of blood through her eardrums.

She was left alone in the darkness, with the flashlight and her phone lying in the snow somewhere. There was no way she was going outside to try and find them.

White tendrils of cold air curled in the chilled atmosphere of the car. *You crazy, careless woman*, she berated herself.

She was in an unfamiliar place, in the dark, and in bad weather. For a moment she was paralyzed. Fear chilled every muscle in her body. She had never in her entire life done anything so rash before. Everything she did was calculated, well-thought out, planned. Except that tonight she'd made a spur-of-the-moment decision and she'd left home in a rush.

She'd put her life in danger.

Dylan was a hundred miles away. At best, he would call her parents. This thought set off another panic inside her. The last thing she wanted was for him to tell her parents. Her mother would be hysterical. And Chloe…

She tried to reassure herself. Maybe there was a chance that they would have called roadside assistance.

I'm going to be fine, she told herself.

Dylan was a sensible man. He would do the right thing, whether that entailed telling her parents or not. Either way, she was sure he would send help.

But what if help took time to find her?

Could she risk sitting here for hours, and dying of hypothermia?

No.

She couldn't die.

She was the only parent Chloe had left. If something

happened to her, Chloe would have no parents. The thought sent chills down her spine.

She. Could. Not. Die.

∼

Fear gnawed in his gut, and he blamed himself. He was worried. Extremely worried. The thought of Merry out in the snow, a hundred miles from here, stranded with a broken-down car left him worried and afraid.

She should never have left and not in that car. He blamed himself as he sprang into action, moving quickly and methodically, putting together everything he needed—a thick blanket, an extra coat, his phone and two battery packs, some food. He even made up a quick Thermos of hot coffee.

He blamed himself for what had happened. He should have checked her car. He should have insisted on it. If he had, Merry wouldn't be stuck out there with her life in danger.

She was in the worst situation—with a broken-down car and in adverse weather conditions. Add a third, in the middle of a place she barely knew.

He would get to her, though.

He would find her.

But it made him wonder how she had missed the weather warnings? The snow had been heavy since late afternoon and there had been reports on TV that the weather was worsening.

In less than fifteen minutes, he was packed, and just before midnight, in the falling snow, he set off in his pickup.

He estimated that it could take anywhere up to two hours to reach her, maybe a little longer, in the worst-case scenario. As much as he wanted to floor the gas pedal, he had to drive carefully because of the snow. It was beyond frustrating. He wanted to speed the whole way there because the thought of

Merry out there in the snow, feeling scared and fearful, made him want to drive like the devil to hell, but he was forced to slow down.

He tried to reassure himself, telling himself that she would be safe out there. It was almost Christmas, and people would be traveling along that route, but she'd said she was in a pull-off. He'd looked on his map, knew the gas station, and had driven through Springfield before. He had an idea where she might be.

It was just a matter of getting there.

CHAPTER 28

*H*e had been driving for almost two hours, and he was getting increasingly worried. Snow fell thicker and thicker on the roads. He feared he wouldn't even be able to find Merry's car if it was covered in snow.

As he neared the place he assumed she would be, his hopes soared, then dove as quickly. He drove along the stretch of road where he expected to find her car, but seeing nothing there, his hopes plummeted. A new type of worry gnawed into his bones. Gnawed into and settled inside his stomach like a worm.

What if she had been here, and he'd been too late? What if someone had driven past...and....and...he couldn't bear to think about it. Already blaming himself, and angry with worry, he drove right past the stretch of road he thought she might be at, and drove around aimlessly, desperate to find her.

What if she'd crashed the car? His stomach spiraled at the thought and he floored the gas pedal. He raced through the snow, not caring anymore, until he reached the gas station where she claimed to have been. This time, he set off, mirroring her journey as she had explained it to him; trying to get inside her head and think like she might have done. It would have been dark, with treacherous snow-covered roads. She had been driving for hours and ... and maybe she didn't turn left after the sign for Springfield? What if she turned right instead, towards Cobalt Springs?

It was worth a try.

He drove on, his hopes resurfacing as he continued down the quiet road. It was almost pitch-dark here, and his level of fear for Merry's safety increased tenfold. She was nowhere near *anything*. No buildings, no houses, no shops or gas stations. If she came down here, she was driving through miles of countryside.

It wasn't a good place to break down in. With only his headlights throwing light in front of him, he turned off the interstate, and scanned around in sheer desperation, wanting, willing, praying for signs of her Jeep Cherokee.

He thought of Chloe, and Merry's parents, and wondered how he would tell them if he didn't find her tonight.

The police.

He would have to call the police. Alert the highway patrol.

And then, just when his hopes couldn't sink any deeper, he saw something along the pull-off area. Something that didn't resemble a bush or a hedge. With his headlights on full beam, he peered closer, craning his neck towards the window as he slowly drove towards it, trying to get a better glimpse. He saw the outline of what looked like a Jeep. It was parked haphazardly, and at an angle, and looked as if it had just been abandoned.

Alarm bells went off in his head.

His heart stopped at the sight of it.

He prayed it was *her* Jeep.

It was covered in inches of snow. While he was relieved he had found her, he was also scared of what he might find inside.

Sweat broke out along the back of his neck just as a surge of adrenaline crashed through his body. What if Merry wasn't inside? Pulling up alongside it, he jumped out and rushed to open the driver's side door. But he couldn't open it.

"Merry!" he shouted, hastily wiping the snow from the window with his gloved hands.

"Merry! It's me, Dylan." He peered in, and saw her head had fallen forward, saw the furry bobble of her hat. He knocked on the window. "Merry!" he yelled, knocking again, yelling even louder. In sheer desperation he took off his glove and knocked with his bare fist.

She looked up, then screamed.

She'd fallen through the ice. It was cold, cold, cold, and the glassy water cut into her skin. But there was a sound.

A banging noise, and she thought she heard someone call out her name. Her eyelids flickered open, and she looked up, and heard the banging, then saw a man's face peering in at her. He was shouting, and she was terrified. She screamed, backing away from the door, frightened for her life.

She screamed even louder, and he banged at the window again, this time with his bare fist.

And then her heart exploded.

Did he say *Dylan?*

She peered closer, her ears only now recognizing the voice, and her eyes slowly starting to focus through the haze of her disorientation.

Dylan.

It was Dylan.

Her Dylan.

Dylan from the store, from the town square, from the woods. Dylan with the tender, tender lips.

He'd found her.

She unlocked the car door, and he pulled it open.

"Thank goodness you're okay!" he cried, reaching in with his big, strong arms. She leaned forward, found herself stuck, her body cold and unmoving, and her face so cold, she couldn't feel it.

And then she found herself shaking.

"I've got you," he said, helping her out, taking her arms and supporting her body against his. "I've got you." He gently pulled her all the way out. She blinked, and hoped that this wasn't a dream, that this was real.

"I—I—" She wanted to speak, but she couldn't move her lips to formulate the words.

"Shush," he told her, when she struggled to stand and instead collapsed against him. His thick arms wrapped around her, and she held onto him, unable to put her arms around him properly. Her body was cold and stiff, and she could barely feel her limbs. He pressed her against him, and she willingly nestled against his neck.

"Cold," she muttered.

"I know," he said, moving his head away. He picked her up easily and walked with her in his arms. "Let's get you into my pickup." He slowly helped her into his pickup, but this time he didn't put her in the front. He put her in the longer seat behind.

She rubbed her hands together, watching him as he rushed into the front and turned the engine on, then put the lights and the heater on before coming to her side again.

He took off her gloves, helped her out of her coat, and gave her his big, warm gloves and a thick jacket. It was warm, and she immediately felt the cold start to dissipate. He draped a blanket over her then pulled out a Thermos and poured something into a cup.

He did all of this silently. She shivered, trying to make sense of it all, of the time of night it was, of the fact that he was here, that he had driven a hundred miles in the snow, this late, and had found her.

"Here," he said, holding the cup to her, "It's hot, take a sip." She couldn't move her hands as easily, so he moved the cup to her lips. "Drink," he ordered softly, and she did. The hot, bitter coffee went down her throat and warmed her insides.

She took her gloves off, *his gloves*, and took the cup from him, letting the warmth heat her hands. "Th..th..thannk...you...," she stuttered, her teeth chattering even though her body was starting to warm up.

"Shush. Don't try to talk. Get warm first. Drink up."

She complied, and drank all the coffee, then held onto the cup, taking all of its warmth.

"Want some more?" he asked.

She shook her head and wrapped the blanket tightly around her. He sat back in the seat. "Come here," he said, "Lean your back against me, so that I can hug you. It will give you more of my body heat. I'm not making a move, I swear."

He took the cup from her as she moved into a comfortable position, with her legs out in front along the seat, and her back against his side. He rubbed her hands with his, warming them faster than any gloves could have, then hugged her, gently rubbing his hands up and down her arms. It was coming back to her now, the feeling in her body, the nerve endings and blood slowly starting to function.

"Better?" he asked, after a while.

She felt the color returning to her cheeks. "Much better. I'm so glad you found me."

"I wasn't going to leave until I did."

"Dylan..."

He stopped rubbing her arms.

"Thank you."

"Don't thank me, Merry. I wouldn't have forgiven myself if something had happened to you."

It didn't make sense to her, that he was blaming himself, but she would ask him about that comment another time. "I fell asleep," she told him. "I didn't mean to, but I just did." She realized she could have slipped into hypothermia.

"You were cold. I'm just thankful that you're okay."

She took his hand and kissed it, overcome by emotion. "I could have die—"

He sat forward, swinging his body slightly so that he could see her face; he tilted her face towards him so that they were looking at one another, and then he reached for her hand. "You didn't die. I wasn't going to leave you out here. I was always going to find you. Don't think about it," he said. "Don't." But she couldn't help it, couldn't help thinking how lucky it had been that she had called him first and not roadside assistance. He touched her cheek lightly with his fingers, then cleared his throat. "I'm not … making a move there…I'm checking to see if you've warmed up."

"I'm…I'm getting warmer. Don't leave me."

"I won't ever leave you. Now, sit back." He sat back himself, and motioned for her to rest against him like before, and she did. This time she sank into him, letting her body go completely soft and meld against his.

"Your mom said you were coming home tomorrow afternoon."

"I heard. She…she's been chatting to you."

"I wouldn't call it chatting so much."

"An interro—terrogation."

He made a low sound in the back of this throat. "I wouldn't call it that, either."

"What then?"

"She was just looking out for you."

"What did she say?" Now she was really curious. Her body was starting to thaw, and loosen, and Dylan's continued rubbing, and his body heat, were doing wonders in warming her up.

"Nothing much," he said, being completely vague. "But she didn't think you were coming home until just in time for the pageant. How come you came back early?"

"I missed …it."

"It?"

"Chloe and … being in…in… Starling Bay." Her teeth were still chattering, but not so much now.

"Chloe and Starling Bay," he said slowly, repeating her words. It was almost as if he was thinking them over, doubting them, examining them.

"You came to get me."

"Are you really that surprised?"

"I'm not used to it. I've had to fend for myself for so…so… long and…and… I'm not used to depending on anyone."

"You can count on me, friends or no friends, Starling Bay or Boston."

She didn't realize it but they had been holding hands. Or rather, his arms were around her, and somehow she was holding *his* hands. They were warm and soft, and they made her feel safe.

"Nice of you to say."

"I mean it."

"That's still a nice thing to say."

They sat quietly, she unsure of what to do now, or how things would be between them.

He broke the silence first. "Are you warm enough?"

"Yes," but she wasn't ready to move away from him. She wasn't quite ready to peel herself away from the warmth of his body.

"Then stay here with the blanket. Do you want another cup of coffee?"

"No, thanks. I'm nice and toasty." She could easily stay here all night.

"Okay, good. I'm going to take a quick look at your car and see if I can fix it." He made to move away slowly.

He was going to do what?

She leaned forward, disliking the idea. "But it's snowing, and it's dangerous out there."

"My point exactly. Whatever were you thinking setting off from Boston on such a long journey at this time of night?"

"I wanted to surprise Chloe," she replied, twisted her body and planting her feet on the floor. She pulled the blanket up around her shoulders.

"Didn't you consider flying? It would have been safe—" He cut off suddenly, and looked at her. "I'm sorry. I didn't mean—"

"It's okay. I need to get over that fear. It would make things easier."

"You're safe now. That's all that matters. I want to look at your car."

"Now?"

"It won't take long, I promise. Where are the keys?"

"In the car, but I don't want to drive it back even if you fix it." That sounded pathetic and whiny, but she didn't care. She would rather stay here in his car and drive back with him.

"You're not driving back. It's too dangerous on the road. The driving conditions are deadly." He went to reach for the door handle.

"There's something out there," she warned. The rustling noise nearby had almost frightened her to death.

He laughed. "There's nothing out there."

"I heard it. Something in the trees. I heard footsteps."

"It was probably a moose or something. It's not uncommon around here."

She hadn't thought of that.

"I can take care of myself, Merry. Where's your phone?"

"Outside. I dropped it when I heard the noise."

He nodded, as if understanding something. "That scared me to death, seeing the car like that. I thought—never mind what I thought. I'm going to check out your car, and find your phone if I can."

"Don't worry about my phone. Just hurry back."

"I will, I promise. Don't move."

She wasn't planning on going anywhere.

CHAPTER 29

"Wake up, sleepyhead." Merry rubbed her eyes.

"We're here, Merry."

She smiled with her eyes still closed. "Are we?" She was waking up to the sound of Dylan's voice; this had to be a dream.

And then her eyelids flew up, and she sat up, straight as a pencil, jolted by the shock.

The light was on, and he was looking at her from the driver's seat, a smirk decorating his lips. "Sleep well?"

"Why didn't you wake me?" she cried, rubbing the side of her neck as she slowly sat up. She must have slept funny, because her neck was hurting a little.

"You were snoring away. Sounded to me like you were in deep sleep."

"I do not snore!"

He nodded, the smirk deepening. "You do."

She pressed her face into her hands. Goodness. No! She prayed she hadn't been drooling.

"But it wasn't very loud, and you were so out of it, I didn't want to wake you."

The thought of him having to listen to her snoring all the way back made her want to curl up and die of embarrassment. "I'm sorry you had to make that horrendous journey back alone." She shifted in the seat and the blanket fell to her waist. Here she was, snuggled up in his car, in *his* blanket and wearing *his* jacket.

Dylan had come through for her.

She didn't want to think what might have happened if he hadn't turned up to rescue her.

"I wasn't alone. I had you in the back."

"You're too modest," she said, looking out of the window to get her bearings. He had parked right outside her house. *Hyacinth's house*, she reminded herself. It was Hyacinth's home in which she had stayed for free in exchange for business experience and know-how.

And she had come away with something that money couldn't buy.

Dylan was a diamond for the keeping.

Not that she would have admitted to it before, but he had been one of the reasons that she had returned to Starling Bay early. Mostly for Chloe, but …a tiny bit for him.

This encounter now put a new light on her feelings for him, uncovering them in a way that was impossible to ignore. She was faced with the truth— raw and exposed—that Dylan meant more to her than she wanted to own up to.

"What time is it?" she asked, suddenly.

"It's 4:15 a.m."

She was horrified. "You've got your pageant today."

"I'll go home and sleep, don't worry about me. The show's not until this evening."

"I'm so sorry I put you out." She felt awful. At 4:15 a.m.*?*

"Don't," he warned with a smile. "Don't apologize. That's what friends do for one another."

Friends? She stared into those twinkling eyes.

"By the way, as far as the problem with your Jeep goes, your fuel injector nozzles were plugged."

"I see." Though she didn't really. She didn't have a clue what a fuel injector nozzle did, or what it looked like.

"I couldn't fix it, and it will need a new part."

"A new part?" She'd have to call someone tomorrow to take a look, and tow it back to Starling Bay where she could hopefully get it fixed.

"Don't worry about it," he said when she frowned. "I'll take care of it."

"How?"

"Don't worry about it."

It was too late to discuss that now. She got out, wearing his way-too-big jacket. "Keep it on," he told her, getting out to accompany her to the door.

"You don't have to walk me to the door," she said. He had already done more than enough.

"I want to make sure you get inside safely."

"You could have watched me from there," she said, indicating towards it with a flick of her chin.

"I'd rather stand here and watch you walk in."

She got out her keys. "Are you always so cautious?" she asked, easing the door open slowly, so as not to make any noise. But it was too late. Spartacus was up and barking with excitement as soon as she walked in.

"Spart!" she hissed, both delighted to see him and wary of waking everyone up.

"Who's there?" her father shouted from the top of the stairs.

"Shhhh. It's only me, dad," she said, stepping into the hallway.

"What in the blazes do you call this?" he asked, coming down in his pajamas.

"Is that you, Meredith?" Her mother's voice floated down the stairs.

"Oh, god, no," Merry mumbled under her breath. She looked at Dylan and gave him an apologetic look. Before she could tell her mother to go back to bed, her father had seen Dylan outside and asked him what the devil he was doing there waiting in the snow. "Come in, young man."

"No, I—"

"Come in, you're letting the cold in," her father insisted. Spartacus nuzzled up to Merry as they all stood, crammed into the small hallway at long after four in the morning.

"Meredith!" her mom shrieked, the tails of her lilac gown floating behind her as she came sailing down the stairs. "Dylan? What the—"

"I can explain," said Merry, although she wasn't in the mood to. So much for her surprising them all by making pancakes for breakfast. "My car broke down and—"

"Broke down?" Her father thundered. "Where?"

"Not far," said Merry, eyeing Dylan in the hope that he wouldn't say anything. Her parents would be furious if they found out what had really happened and in what danger she might have been had Dylan not come to her rescue.

"Come into the kitchen," said her mother, reaching for Dylan's arm, "And I'll make everyone a hot drink."

"Mother," said Merry tightly. "It's late, or early, and Dylan is tired, and so am I. Let's not make a commotion and wake Chloe up."

"That's a good idea," said Dylan, moving outside again. "I should go. Thank you, anyway."

Her mother looked disappointed.

"Dad, Mom, why don't you both get back to bed?" Merry started to usher her parents off. "I'm here now, I'm safe. I wanted to surprise everyone, but things didn't go according to plan."

"I suppose you are here and safe," said her father.

"Thanks to Dylan," her mother countered.

"Let's get to bed, Irene." Her father marched her mother upstairs again.

Merry turned to Dylan who was still standing outside, his hair flecked with cotton-candy tufts of snow. "Thanks, again," she said.

"I'd have done it for anyone."

That made it not sound so great. It put a dampener on things. "That's a lie, actually," he said, leaning against the doorframe. "Not *anyone*. Nobody but you is worth driving out at midnight for."

She smiled at him. A genuine, full-on, hundred-watt light bulb smile. "And I would rather be rescued by you than anyone else."

"Yeah?" he asked, sounding casual.

"Most definitely yes."

His lips twisted, and he made a peculiar face as if he was about to say something, but in the end he settled for putting his hands into his jean pockets. "That's nice to hear," he said eventually.

"All that other stuff I said? Before I went away...that doesn't count anymore." Before he had a chance to respond, she leaned in, and tiptoed up to him, leaving a soft kiss on his lips. His brows pushed together slightly. "I'd make it a proper one," she said, "but I'm all horrible and smelly and ..."

He laid his lips on her forehead; a gentle and quick press of the lips, and gave her a smile that said many things yet still left her wondering. "I'll see you later today, at the pageant?" he asked.

"I wouldn't miss it for anything."

CHAPTER 30

*H*e hadn't slept well. How could he, when all he kept thinking about was Merry, and what she had said to him? *All that other stuff I said? Before I went away... that doesn't count anymore.*

He didn't dare to think about what it might mean. Didn't dare to raise his hopes. Even if they did get together, how would it be? In what capacity could they be together when she lived in Boston and he was here?

His last girlfriend left him because she got fed up of Starling Bay and hankered for the city life. Merry was from the city. She had a great career. How could he ever hope to compete with that?

What they had shared was a brief encounter. Kissing in the snow did not a relationship make. For him it had been the prelude to wanting more. But what did this mean for Merry? He had no idea.

With broken sleep making things worse, he woke up a couple of hours later and asked Laura to come in early.

"You look rough," Laura commented. "Are you nervous about the pageant?"

The pageant.

He'd forgotten about the pageant. He'd been too busy trying to figure out what to do about Merry's Jeep.

It was at times like this that knowing Reed Knight was especially helpful.

"Mom!" Chloe was on the bed, hugging her. "Mom, you came back!"

Woken with a jolt, Merry sat up, not minding that her daughter was almost squashing her. "You said you weren't coming until later."

"I had a change of plans. I didn't want to miss any of it, and I thought it would be nice wandering around the square beforehand, so you could buy all your last-minute Christmas presents."

Spartacus lay on the floor, looking up at them both longingly.

"Grandma says Dylan brought you home."

"Did she now?" Merry wondered what else her mother might have said, or might have been thinking.

"What happened?" Chloe asked.

"I broke down in the middle of nowhere, honey, and I called Dylan, and he came and got me."

"He's the best."

"He is."

Chloe looked down at her hands.

"What's wrong?" Merry asked.

"Nothing."

"Chloe?"

"Don't you want to do the pageant?" Merry asked, thinking it might be nerves.

"It's all going to be over soon."

"And?"

"And then we have to go home, don't we?"

"Eventually."

"I like it here."

Merry knew that feeling. "It's nice here," she admitted. Her perception of the town had changed. A month ago her mother had had to coerce her into coming here, yet last night she had set off late at night and in bad weather, because she couldn't wait to get back.

"Can't we stay longer?"

Merry opened her mouth. She had already decided that, hadn't she? When she'd walked away from Shepworth's pre-Christmas cocktail party? She'd started to wonder, albeit in a roundabout way, of leaving Boyd & Meyer. It would mean having to leave her comfort zone, and venture out into the unknown. Should she stay, or should she go? Could she continue the way she had before, not being there for Chloe and giving her all to Boyd & Meyer? Could she sustain that type of life? Did she want to?

Having known a world with Dylan in it, could she go back to a world without him?

But even if she did come back for a vacation, or somehow find a way to have him in her life, what if things didn't work out? What then?

Was she willing to take the chance and try?

"Grandma says Dylan likes you but you're too stubborn to see it."

"She said that?"

"And I saw you two holding hands." Chloe's eyes blazed back at her.

Merry opened her mouth, recalling that time at the rehearsals. After the walk in the woods.

"I don't want you to get sick again, Mom." Chloe's arms went around her, and she buried her face in Merry's shoulder.

This was new. She hadn't realized that it had affected her daughter so much. "Honey," she said softly, moving back so that she could look at Chloe's face. "Sweetie." She lifted Chloe's face gently. "I'm not planning on getting sick again. I'm going to slow down and take care of myself, so that I can take care of you and me."

"What about Dylan? Grandma said he took care of you last night and it was about time you gave that poor man a chance."

Merry couldn't help but suppress her smile. Chloe had said those words verbatim as if they had come out of her mother's mouth. "Do you like Dylan?"

Chloe nodded. "He's really nice, and he's really kind, and he's always making sure I'm having fun."

"I like him, too, honey." And she was going to tell him at the performance today. "What time is it?" she asked, cradling Chloe in her arms.

"Two o'clock."

"Two o'clock?!" Merry screamed. Why hadn't anyone woken her up? "I need to get up. You have the pageant, Chloe!" Merry screamed.

Chloe sensed her mother's shock. "What's the worst that could happen, Mom? And Grandma said to let you sleep."

Merry stifled a smile. Dylan's laidback attitude was contagious. "I was supposed to make pancakes and surprise you all."

"You *did* surprise me by being here."

"Aww, honey." Merry hugged Chloe to her chest again. Coming home early had been worth it for this.

Spartacus sprang up and bolted out of the room—something he did whenever there was food or someone at the door.

"I'll go and see who it is." Chloe sprang off the bed at breakneck speed. Merry scrambled out of bed, hating the fact that she had slept in so late, but the sound of Dylan's voice floated to her ears. She stopped and listened in the doorway, straining to hear. They were talking; Chloe, and Dylan, and her mother.

"She's upstairs," she heard Chloe say. "She just got up."

Merry panicked. She hadn't brushed her teeth, and she was in her pajamas, and bra-less, and she looked like death. *Goodness, no!* Dylan wouldn't come up to see her, would he?

She raced around the room, sliding on a sweatshirt, and lounge pants, and then heard a knock on her bedroom door. She didn't want to turn around.

"That was Dylan," said her mother, walking in and sitting on the bed.

"He's gone?" Her heart sank.

"He came to see how you were and to let us know that your car is getting fixed at the garage. It should be ready to pick up later this evening."

"He managed to get my car towed back a hundred miles and dropped off at a garage?" *On Christmas Eve, while she had been sleeping?* And he had a performance this evening?

"He's…" she couldn't think of all the words that came to her. "He's amazing and so thoughtful."

"He's exactly the type of man you need," replied her mother. "And I suggest you snap him up before someone else does."

"Mother!"

"Someone's got to tell you, Meredith."

"I know what I need to do, Mom." And the first of it was getting over to the town square early, so that she could walk around with Chloe, and help Dylan set up for the show.

CHAPTER 31

*I*t was going to be a beautiful disaster. He expected the usual, unpredictable things to go wrong with the show, but he hadn't expected Leah to call him this morning and tell him she hadn't been able to adjust the costumes, even though she'd had over a week to do them.

He didn't care.

He suspected there was more to it than her saying she had a cold. And Merry had called him earlier. After thanking him for getting her car fixed, she'd offered to come over early and help him set up. He didn't want anyone to tread on Chloe's toes; she was in charge of the setup, but he'd explained to Merry about his costume mishap and she told him she would take care of it.

And here she was with a sewing basket, ready to get to work.

"You came equipped," he said, warming to the sight of her. It had been a mad dash to get her Jeep back, but Reed had called in a favor from a local garage, and sent one of the guys to tow it back. They were going to work on it and would have it fixed within a few hours. He hadn't been able to sleep, so making use of that time and doing *something* felt better than trying to get some sleep.

Merry set down her basket and walked towards him, making him suddenly conscious of his disheveled appearance. He ran his palm across his chin, feeling the hairs all across his jaw. There had been no time to shave.

She tiptoed up and pressed her lips against his.

"That's a great way to say 'hello'. Do it again," he begged.

She shook her head, and lifted her face to his, this time pressing her lips against his for a moment longer. Fire ignited inside him. "What was that for?" Not that he minded.

"For sorting out my car, for having it towed back and dropped off at a garage." She stared up at him, gratitude written all over her face. "But how did you manage it? It was a hundred miles away."

He shrugged. "Couldn't leave it there, and couldn't wait for roadside assistance to do it, given that you weren't near the car."

"I wouldn't even have known who to call."

"I told you I'd take care of it."

"And you did," she murmured.

"I called in a few favors. I know that you're going to need it soon, what with you going back home and all." He tried to read her expression, tried to get a hint of what she might be thinking.

"Maybe not so soon. I'm still signed off from work on medical leave for another month."

"Another month, huh?" He put his hands around her waist. A month was a start.

She touched his stubble, her soft hand moving across his jawline. "Did you even sleep?"

"Not much. I had to do something with my energy."

"You've already done so much for me."

He pulled her closer, stared down into those amber colored eyes of hers and basked in the sunshine of her smile. "I'd do it all over again. For you, I'd do anything."

She rewarded him with a kiss. "I'll get started with those costume adjustments as soon as I peel myself away from you."

"You can't. We're stuck together, like glue."

"Feels good," she murmured, tilting her head up. He kissed her again. Her body was warm and soft against his, and holding her like this did things to his breathing. He had to step away before things got too heated between them. She seemed to have the same thought, because she moved away at the same time. "I'd better get to those adjustments," she said, looking slightly flustered.

"Good idea." They had a month. A month was a beautiful start.

She had expected to cringe and hide her face in embarrassment. She had expected to feel embarrassed for the children, but the show had worked out surprisingly well.

Dylan had been worried for no reason.

And Chloe, even though she hadn't been on stage, seemed years older, taking on the responsibility for everything behind the scenes.

Merry had sat with her parents and Hyacinth in the front row of the tiny area where chairs had been laid out. It was cold, but here in this corner of the Square, it didn't *feel* cold, even though her mother complained about it. Merry was basking in the glow of her memories with Dylan. Of the behind-the-scene kisses, and of what the future might bring.

The performance had ended with a rapturous applause which —with her mom and dad leading the way—had turned into a standing ovation.

Hyacinth beamed with overdone enthusiasm. "The children were magnificent!"

"It was brilliant!" Merry agreed.

"He's a natural, that Dylan Fraser," Hyacinth continued. "That's why I force him to do it every year, because he always brings out the best in the children."

Merry wondered if this would be Dylan's last show, and if he would be able to turn down Hyacinth next year. Would she be here next year? The idea that had once seemed so far-fetched suddenly didn't seem all that crazy.

"Did you like it, Mom?" Chloe cried excitedly as she rushed towards her.

"I loved it!"

"Did you?" Chloe asked her grandparents.

"It was amazing."

"I know I wasn't on the stage this time—"

"You were. We saw you rushing around getting things ready for each scene."

"Next year I might audition for a part."

"Now that is a splendid idea," her Grandma agreed.

"You go ahead with Grandma and Grandpa," Merry told Chloe. "I'll see you around the square. Let me help Dylan tidy up."

Chloe stared back at her with shining eyes. "Take your time, Mom. I'm buying both your presents, so I don't want you to come around with me."

"Okay," Merry replied, knowingly. She started to clear up while people were still congratulating Dylan on the show. Folding the discarded costumes, she stopped for a moment and looked out at the square, then at the tree in the center, its jeweled lights sparkling in the darkness like a beacon of merriment. Glancing at the people milling around, and seeing the Christmas stalls set in the distance, Merry was overcome by a feeling of belonging.

Of wanting to belong.

Of falling in love with Starling Bay.

She could picture herself living here.

Not only that, but she didn't feel alone any more, not with Dylan by her side, helping her, supporting her and being there for her for as long as she wanted. She had forgotten what it was like, to have someone like that in her life.

The moment brought a lump to her throat, because it was an acknowledgment of the past and the door she was closing on it, and the possibility of a future that was both unknown and exciting.

She wandered behind the set, and busied herself packing the costumes away.

"There you are." Dylan's voice behind her jolted her. She turned around.

"I was cleaning up."

He walked over to her, and touched her cheek gently. "Was it that bad?" he asked, looking at her face, concerned.

"Bad?"

"Tell me the truth. What did you think?"

"It was really good, Dylan. Really, *really* good."

"Then why do you look so upset?"

"I'm not upset. I'm…I'm overwhelmed."

He frowned. "I didn't think the show would have had that much of an impact on you."

"The show was brilliant," she insisted, smiling because he had that effect on her. He made her smile. Always.

"Thank you." He cupped her face.

"I've realized how much I like this."

"The show?"

"All of this. You, and Starling Bay, and Chloe—she's so happy here."

"And you?"

"I'm happy because you make me happy."

That seemed to stump him, and for a moment he said nothing. "That's funny you should say that," he said, taking a lock of her hair and rubbing it between his fingers. "Because you make *me* happy. I'm hoping that this Christmas might be different for you, that you won't hate it as much."

"It's been different."

"Different," he mused, then dipped his head so that their noses touched. She closed her eyes, reveling in the closeness of him, and the feel of his skin on hers. It awoke in her a sense of deep yearning she hadn't felt in years. He kissed her again, his electric touch setting off tiny fireworks in her stomach.

It had been a long time coming, this awakening, but with him it was core-deep.

"Look at you lovebirds hiding behind the scenes."

They pulled apart.

Rourke had a smile plastered on his face.

"You found them," said Reed, appearing a few seconds later.

"And look what I found. I caught them in the act."

Dylan groaned, but held onto her hand as they both faced his friends who looked as if they'd won a multi-million-dollar lottery. "This has to be a Christmas miracle, seeing Dylan with a—"

Reed jabbed Rourke in the ribs.

"You'll get used to him and his big mouth," Dylan told her.

"I'm the more sensible one of the two, though you probably already knew that," said Reed.

"I guessed," Merry replied, smiling.

"So, uh, now that we found you, I guess we'll just see you around the square," said Rourke.

"Be there in ten," Dylan replied. "And thanks for the car," he said to Reed.

"*You* fixed the car?" Merry asked.

Dylan laughed. "Reed didn't fix your car. He couldn't fix a

busted lightbulb. This guy doesn't get his hands dirty, but he knows plenty of people who will."

"Well, thank you, anyway," said Merry.

"He's got contacts coming out of his ears," explained Dylan.

"It really wasn't too hard to make a few phone calls," Reed told her.

"But it's Christmas Eve and I appreciate that it can't have been easy."

"Is Olivia here?" Dylan asked, looking around.

"Don't ask."

"What do you mean *don't ask*?"

Reed's face darkened. "Just that." He smiled at Merry, his countenance changing suddenly. "We'll see you around the square."

When they left, she questioned Dylan. "What was all that about?"

"I'm not so sure anymore. He has a lot going on, running all those businesses and having so much responsibility. It can't be easy."

"No family?"

"His parents moved to Montana, bought a ranch and a million horses," he chuckled. "And Reed's an only child. He's from one of the oldest and richest families in Starling Bay, and he knows everyone."

"That's why he's got all the contacts?"

"Exactly. He's also supposed to be getting married soon. Oh, I forgot to tell you, we're invited to their New Year's Eve party at his mansion, if it's still going ahead, that is."

"A New Year's Eve party?" Merry asked.

"He told me to bring a friend."

"A friend?"

"You'll do."

She poked him in the ribs gently. "That's good to know. Friends is good, it's a starting point."

"Except that friends don't kiss like we do," he whispered into her ear.

She giggled, maybe even blushed a little. "It's not as scary as I thought it would be, this...getting to know someone all over again."

"This is new for me, too." He stroked her face, and she wished he would leave his hand there. It was more than a gesture, more than a casual expression of his feelings. It was comfort, and security, and being wanted. "I don't know what the future holds, Merry, but I'm willing to give *us* a try, if you are."

"I like the sound of *us*."

He looked into her eyes. "When you're around, you make it seem as if anything is possible."

"Anything?"

"And everything."

She nodded, knowing, and understanding, because she felt the same.

"I feel as if you and me, we could be something together. Not just the two of us, but you and me, and Chloe, and that great big humongous elephant-beast dog of yours."

She laughed. "I'm pleased you remembered him."

"He's hard to forget. As are you." He thumbed her lower lip. She loved hearing him say all these things, as much as she loved whatever it was he was doing to her lip, and her skin, and her senses. She shivered, not from the cold, but from the anticipation of what the future with him might hold.

"It'll be okay, won't it?" she asked, because the future was uncertain, as much as it was scary and exciting.

"Yes," he said, full of confidence. "Things didn't work out for you, and they didn't for me either, but we found each other, didn't we?"

She nodded, overcome by so much emotion that she was unable to speak.

"This feels right, for me it does," he continued. "Does it for you?"

It absolutely did. She hadn't come to Starling Bay expecting to find anything, let alone *anyone*. But she had found exactly what she needed. "It feels perfect." She snuggled against his shoulder, not wanting to move. He held her close, and they stayed like that for a few moments.

"Chloe and my parents are probably looking for us," she said, after a while.

"And Reed and Rourke are waiting around the town square. We should get going."

"We should."

He reached for her hand, getting ready to walk around the square. "Are you up for it, Merry? All that Christmas spirit?"

Yes, she was, because, suddenly, Christmas wasn't so bad anymore.

Thank you for reading ***Winter's Kiss!*** I hope you enjoyed Dylan and Merry's story. If you want to know how their story concludes, you can find out in ***Winter's Vow***, which is Book 5 in the ***Starling Bay series***.

If you're intrigued about Reed and Rourke, fear not! **They have their own stories, too.**

Reed's book, ***Maid for Him***, is now available! You can read a first chapter excerpt at the end of this book.

. . .

If you enjoyed *Winter's Kiss*, and if you have a moment to spare and it's not too much trouble, please consider leaving a review at Goodreads or Amazon. **A review can be as short as one sentence, and your opinion goes a long way in helping others decide if a book is for them.**

Thank you,

Sienna

EXCERPT FROM MAID FOR HIM

Chapter 1

"*P*lease, Shay. I need something quick and easy. Something I can start today," Jenna pleaded.

"I know. I heard you. I heard you last night, and the day you arrived, Jenna. But you don't have to follow me into work." Her friend looked at her and made a face. Jenna felt useless, worse, she was beginning to feel like a burden. Returning to Starling Bay had seemed like a good idea a few weeks ago when she'd been sitting in her cockroach-infested room in a shared apartment, eating ramen noodles.

She had decided that enough was enough. Between working at the supermarket, and working as a waitress in the evenings, she barely had much money left over, and what she did have, she saved.

Starling Bay seemed like heaven, and it offered a new lease of life, and that was enough for her to pack her bags and return after twelve years.

But now that she had been here a few weeks, the doubts started to creep in. It wasn't a city, and didn't offer the job opportunities in such abundance. It wasn't exactly small, either, and it had changed. She didn't remember it being so expensive. Or maybe, she'd been so dirt poor all her life, that *everything* was expensive.

She was here now and she had no choice but to make things work. This was going to be her fresh start, dang it, and there was no going back. "I have no money," she insisted. "And I'm camping out on your sofa. I need to get back on my feet." Her friend had no idea what it was like to be so broke. She had a couple of hundred dollars to her name, and she was going to budget very carefully until she got a job. A *couple* of jobs, she figured, if it came to that.

"Look," said Shay, pushing up her glasses. "It's Monday morning, I need to get back into work mode, check my emails—"

"Please," Jenna begged. She didn't have the time to sit around waiting while Shay 'eased into work mode'. "Please. Can't you take a quick look now and see if anything's come up over the weekend? I'll leave you in peace, I promise." And then she would hound Shay later when she returned home from work in the evening.

Shay huffed out a breath and peered closer at her screen. "I've got a couple of cleaning jobs." She frowned. "Maybe not."

"I'll take it."

"No. I don't think this one is any..." Her friend's voice tapered away, and she moved her mouse pointer around. Jenna wished she could stand over her friend's shoulder and see the screen for herself instead of trying to decipher Shay's facial expressions.

"Whatever it is, I'll take it." She wasn't fussy.

"Ah, here's another one." Shay smiled.

"What is it?"

"Cleaning a group of small offices, or," she peered closer at the screen.

"Or?" asked Jenna, in her mind she had already accepted the first job. "They need a someone to clean for a few hours every morning at the preschool."

"The preschool?" She imagined this would be small and easy enough to do. How much mess did tiny kids make? "What was the first job?" she asked suspiciously. It seemed that there was something Shay wasn't telling her.

"You won't want it."

"You haven't told me what it is yet."

"Trust me. You won't want it."

"Is it cleaning toilets? Because I'll do it." She would do whatever it took.

"It's...uh..." Shay settled back in her seat, and folded her arms. "It's cleaning some rich guy's mansion—"

"I'll do it. Sign me up already."

Shay opened her mouth, and her lips twisted but no words came out. She eyed Jenna with a level gaze.

"How bad can it be? I'll do it."

"It's the Knight mansion."

Those four words had the power to paralyze her. She snorted. "You've got to be kidding me. That thing is still standing?"

"Of course it's still standing."

"And they still live there?" Of course they did. Why would they not? The Knights were as old as the dinosaurs. They'd been here from the start. Generations of Knights had lived in the huge sprawling mansion in Glassmere, the exclusive end of Starling Bay. It was away from the busy town center and the bay, with the back of the house overlooking the ocean.

For her, it represented extreme humiliation and she seethed at the mention of it.

"They don't live here anymore, only Reed does. His parents bought a ranch in Montana."

"They did?" Jenna imagined horses running wild on acres of land. "Why would you buy a ranch in Montana?"

"Because they can. What does it matter to you?"

Jenna shrugged. The lives of the rich were a continent away from her own. She was living with Shay, for now, because she couldn't yet afford to rent a small apartment of her own, and Reed Knight's parents had left an enormous, fit-for-a-king mansion, to go and live on a ranch in Montana. It wouldn't surprise her if they'd bought a thousand-acre ranch out there. The Knights super-sized everything.

"I told you that you wouldn't want this one."

Jenna swallowed. "I'll do it. I'll clean his house." Of all the men she could have run into, and all the places she would end up in, it would have to be this one. "I need it." She really did. Reed Knight or not.

"Is this wise?" Shay asked.

"I need the money, and I will do a good job wherever you put me, but if this is the only position that is available, I'll take it. I'll work at that place, for him." She couldn't even bring herself to say the names. "I hate that they think they're better than us, and I hate that he thinks he can treat the likes of us as if we're—"

"You're still mad at him, Jenna! I'm not sure this is going to work out."

"I'm over it," Jenna said quickly. "It was nothing. He won't even recognize me, not with this." She gently tugged at her hair.

"Would it really be such a problem if he did?"

"I can't stand the guy so—" She stared at Shay, then smiled. "It's not going to be a problem."

"I can't afford to give this to you if there are going to be problems, Jenna."

"I'll be as good as gold, I promise. When can I start?"

"I'll need to check with his PA," said Shay.

"He has a personal assistant?" Jenna scoffed. "I'll bet he has a chauffeur, and a cook, and a gardener, and—."

"He keeps it simple, from what I've heard. He only has his personal assistant, more like a butler, say, and someone to cook for him and a maid to clean."

"The luxury of having these people in your life," Jenna muttered. "He doesn't cook for himself *at all?*"

"The cook's probably been in the family for years, like the butler. He doesn't need to do it, so why should he?"

"It's still surprising that in this day and age, a grown man needs someone to cook for him."

"You really have it out for him, don't you? I'm not sure you working for him is a smart move, for you or for me. I'm not sure I can place you there, Jenna. It would look bad on the agency if you messed up. It would look bad on me."

"I'll be good. I promise." She rushed to reassure her friend. "I'm curious to know what he's like now."

"If you keep your mouth shut, you might get to find out. Did you know he's engaged to be married this summer?"

"Poor woman," Jenna muttered.

"He's not as bad as he used to be."

"Easy enough for you to say."

"I was there that night as well."

Jenna looked away. Reed Knight had helped her up when she'd fallen down on the track one day. One of the most popular boys at the school, he had been polite, and concerned, and she'd been smitten. And when she and her friends had received an invite to his party months later, she'd been beyond excited. But that day had ended in a humiliation that she had carried around with her for years. Nobody had been in her shoes. Yes, Shay had been there with her, but Shay hadn't been the one they had laughed at.

"Let me call his PA and arrange for an interview."

"Can you do it now? I'd like to start as soon as possible."

Chapter 2

∽

The sound of the ringing phone thundered in his ears. Reed reached out to grab it, but knocked the sleek handset off his nightstand instead.

And then his cell phone started ringing, and the noise sliced through his ears like a blade. He winced because his head felt as if it had been axed into two.

"Mr. Pennington?"

"No, it's Reed Knight."

"Oh, I'm sorry to disturb you, Mr. Knight. It's Shay Donovan from the recruitment agency."

"Who?"

"Shay, from the recruitment agency."

What in the blazes were they calling him for? And where was Pennington?

"You were looking to hire a maid?"

"Talk to my PA."

"Mr. Pennington mentioned that he was away on vacation and to contact you directly. He said it was urgent."

Reed groaned, remembering. Trust his entire household staff to abandon him at the same time. "Ugh," he sat up and steadied himself on the bed. The room was spinning. "Can it wait?" he thundered, then winced as his head started to throb.

"Mr. Pennington said he wanted someone to start as soon as possible, and I've found just the right person. She's ready to start as soon as possible."

Reed put a hand to his throat. Inside, it felt parched. He didn't need anyone this week, and he could cope just fine alone.

"Shall I send her over, before she gets assigned somewhere else? You did say you wanted someone quickly?"

"I said nothing of the sort," he growled, standing to his feet and sitting back down again. Did Pennington think he couldn't handle anything by himself? Maybe Olivia, his fiancée, had put him up to it. That princess couldn't cook or clean, or do much else, as he was beginning to find out. He slammed the phone down, and sat back on the bed, resting his back against the headboard.

Going out with his friends hadn't been a good idea. He needed to get a handle on these late nights, but he hadn't seen Dylan and Rourke for weeks, not since the New Year's Eve party which Olivia had insisted on throwing.

What a farce.

He wiped a hand across his brow, thinking about the mess he was in. Some days he wasn't so sure it was pre-wedding nerves. Olivia didn't seem to harbor anything of the sort, and she was certainly an expert when it came to spending his money.

He gulped down half a glass of water and downed two painkillers, then grabbed his cell phone and checked his business emails, all from the comfort of his bed. Work never stopped, no matter what. He also had a few important calls to make, and got started with those.

He paced around the room as he made his calls, and when the doorbell rang, he ignored it automatically.

It wasn't until the doorbell rang for the fourth or fifth time that he remembered Pennington wasn't here, and Cecile, his cook, had gone away to care for her sister who'd had an operation.

"One moment," he said to the person at the other end of the line, then, when the doorbell rang again, "I'll call you right back." Annoyed, Reed quickly pulled on a pair of jeans. "Shouldn't have let him go," he muttered to himself. Damn Pennington and his two-week bird-watching trip to Costa Rica.

He sauntered downstairs and opened the door to find a woman standing on his doorstep. A pair of green eyes stared back at him, but it was her blue-tipped hair that grabbed his attention. "Yes?" he asked, not happy with the interruption because he hated when people wasted his time.

She was obviously here to sell something, because he didn't know who she was, and he hardly ever had visitors.

"I've come for the interview. Shay sent me."

For details of this and other starling bay books, Please visit my website.

http://www.siennacarr.com

BOOKLIST

Whirlwind Kisses

Winter's Kiss

Maid for Him

Love Letters

Escape to Starling Bay (Books 1-3)

From Faking to Forever

Winter's Vow

Guarded Hearts

A Bouquet of Charm

ACKNOWLEDGMENTS

I would like to thank my amazing group of proofreaders who check my manuscript for errors, typos and inconsistencies.

I am eternally grateful for their help and support:

Marcia Chamberlain
Nancy Dormanski
April Lowe
Dena Pugh
Charlotte Rebelein
Carole Tunstall

I would also like to thank Tatiana Vila of Vila Design for creating the awesome cover.

ABOUT THE AUTHOR

Sienna Carr is a pen name for an author who has been writing romance since 2013. She lives in the UK with her husband, three children, and a parrot.

Connect with Me
> I love hearing from you – so please don't be shy!
> You can email me at: sienna@siennacarr.com

Check out my website at:
> http://www.siennacarr.com

Made in the USA
Middletown, DE
01 June 2022

66474395R00146